I0657143

Serial
Killer

...by the book

Serial Killer

...by the book

A Mark Daniels Mystery

Justin Maxwell

ABSOLUTELY AMAZING eBOOKS

ABSOLUTELY AMAZING eBOOKS

Published by Whiz Bang LLC, 926 Truman Avenue, Key West, Florida 33040, USA.

Serial Killer ... by the Book copyright © 2016 by Wayne Kadar. Electronic compilation/ paperback edition copyright © 2016 by Whiz Bang LLC.

All rights reserved. No part of this book may be reproduced, scanned, or transmitted in any form or by any means, electronic or mechanical, including photocopying, recording, or any information storage and retrieval system, without permission in writing from the publisher. Please do not participate in or encourage piracy of copyrighted materials in violation of the author's rights. Purchase only authorized ebook editions.

This is a work of fiction. Names, characters, places, and incidents either are the product of the author's imagination or are used fictitiously, and any resemblance to actual persons, living or dead, businesses, companies, events, or locales is entirely coincidental. While the author has made every effort to provide accurate information at the time of publication, neither the publisher nor the author assumes any responsibility for errors, or for changes that occur after publication. Further, the publisher does not have any control over and does not assume any responsibility for author or third-party websites or their contents. How the ebook displays on a given reader is beyond the publisher's control.

For information contact:
Publisher@AbsolutelyAmazingEbooks.com

ISBN-13:978-1945772153 (Absolutely Amazing Ebooks)
ISBN-10: 1945772158

Serial
Killer

...by the book

Chapter 1

The moon was just a silver sliver in the dark sky as the car slowly pulled off the two-track, turning towards a clearing by the river. The driver got out of the car and quickly closed the door to extinguish the dome light. He looked around and listened for any sign of other people although he didn't expect to find anyone this far off the highway at 4:36 in the morning.

Content that he was alone, the man walked to the rear of the car and opened the trunk. The trunk lamp illuminated the frightened girl who was scrunched in the small compartment, her naked body folded in a fetal position. The woman squinted from the light after being kept in the darkness for almost two hours; she looked up at the man. Duct tape pressed over her mouth prevented her from screaming, plastic wire ties bound her hands behind her back and eyes reddened with tears pleaded with the man not to harm her.

His hand reached in the trunk, grabbed the naked girl by the hair and pulled her up his other hand grabbed a leg and he lifted her out and lowered her to the ground. The man calmly reached down and wrapped his fingers around her throat. The girl looked up into his eyes and made pleading sounds as he tightened his grip and watched her face turn red, her eyes open wide, and the veins at the side of her forehead swell. The girl's body went limp as the man squeezed her neck so tightly his arms trembled

He let go of the girl and her lifeless body fell to the ground. The man reached into the trunk, grabbed a pair of pliers to cut the plastic ties from her wrists and ankles and peeled a corner of the tape covering her mouth, pinched it between his thumb and finger and ripped it off. He tossed the pliers, cut wire ties and piece of tape into the trunk. He smiled at the girl laying at his feet, the girl he met at the bar and had let him know she was available after she got off work, available for a price.

He knelt down on one knee, and pulled the girls' panties from his back pocket and stuffed them in her mouth, using his fingers to shove them down her throat. He stood up and looked at the girl lying at his feet and smiled, proud of his work.

The man took a condom from his pocket, ripped it open tossing the wrapper in the trunk. He kicked her feet apart, unzipped his pants and kneeled between her legs.

When he had fulfilled his perverse desires, the killer reached down, lifted the dead girl over his shoulder and walked to the edge of the river. He gently laid her into the water with a slight splash and gave her a little shove with his foot. The body slowly drifted away from shore.

"Bon voyage," the man said giving the girl a wave as he watched her slip into the darkness.

Chapter 2

Mark lay in bed wondering, "Why do I wake up at 5:17 every morning? I didn't always wake up at 5:17. When I was in college I was lucky if I didn't sleep through my 10:00 classes, but for the last couple of years or so its 5:17 am. Why 5:17? Does it have some significance in my life? Sometimes I can fall back to sleep but I always wake up at 5:17 exactly. Well, at least I didn't have the nightmare last night."

He slowly pulled the covers off, trying not to disturb his wife, although even if he did she would just roll over and fall back to sleep for another couple of hours. The dog, curled at the foot of the bed, didn't even lift its head as he slid out of bed and pulled on his old dark green terry cloth robe. Descending the stairs from the loft, he flicked the wall switch turning on the gas fireplace. By the light of the fire he walked to the kitchen to push the coffee maker on button, and then walked to the bathroom.

It's the same ritual he's followed just about every morning for the last couple years; bathrobe, fireplace, coffee pot, pee, get a cup of coffee, walk to the couch, open the laptop. While the computer warms up he looks out the wall of windows overlooking the lake; in the twilight he can see a duck leaving a small wake as it paddles on water as flat as a mirror, there's just a hint of daylight on the horizon.

Watching the reflection of the fire in the fireplace dancing on the varnished pine boards on the walls and ceiling he thinks, "I wonder how many mornings I have had in my life. How many days have I had in my 66 plus years? It's a simple thing to figure out... but I'll need a calculator."

After his finger pushed a few buttons on his cell phone calculator app he says, "24,191. I have had 24,191 mornings in my life," Mark thought. "More than I expected."

Anyway, back to the morning ritual. First he opens USA Today to see what's happening in the world. Nothing that holds his attention; a suicide bomber blows himself up in Syria while he was assembling a detonator. "Oops," Mark says. An article that says we're still losing the battle of global warming and California is in a drought.

He took a sip of coffee and moved the cursor to the Detroit Free Press app and clicked. "Maybe something is happening in Detroit that's interesting. Let's see; Detroit's mayor is pledging to tear down more vacant houses, the Illich family announces they'll be opening a new restaurant as part of their sprawling downtown sports complex, Dan Gilbert bought another building in downtown, and there was a drug related shooting on Detroit's east side."

A click on the Michigan tab brings a series of articles from all around the state; gas prices expected to rise, a company wants to reopen an iron ore mine in the Upper Peninsula. "That's a good thing," Mark mumbles.

Three and half hours after he walked down from the loft bedroom of their cottage, Mark heard the dog jump off the bed, signaling his wife was waking up and would soon make an appearance. He stood by the front door waiting for the old Yorkie dog to come downstairs and go out for her morning pee and poop. He had to keep an eye on the little eight-pound dog because of the eagle with the nest across the lake and the fox that lived in the area or the small dog could be breakfast.

As Sherry walked down the stairs, Mark looked at his bride of nearly 45 years thinking, "She is still a sexy woman. Well maybe not right now, wearing her old pink robe, and with her hair uncombed and sleep wrinkles on her face giving away the fact that she slept on her left side, but most of the time she is sexy."

"Morning," Sherry said, her slippers making a shuffling sound as she passed, heading towards the bathroom.

"Good morning Sunshine," Mark said cheerfully, his way of rubbing it in that he gets up early and gets his day started and his wife has always been hesitant to welcome a new day.

He let the dog in and it sat outside the bathroom door waiting for Sherry to emerge. It is her dog and she is its human. Mark pours another cup of coffee in his cup and mixes a coffee for his wife; one part black coffee to three parts French Vanilla coffee creamer, and places it next to her chair by the fireplace. He smiles at her as she shuffles into the living room, the dog at her heels.

Sherry sits down, kicks out the footrest and the dog jumps into her lap. "Did you sleep alright? You were restless," Sherry asks. "Did you have the nightmare?"

"Nope, slept soundly until 5:17."

Sherry sips her French Vanilla coffee, absent-mindedly scratches the dog and asked, "Anything in the news?" Sherry knows Mark's morning ritual.

"Nope, same old crap."

Chapter 3

Mark Daniels opened his eyes, and before he checked the alarm clock he knew it would read 5:17 AM. He pulled the blanket up over his head to try to get some more sleep, but it didn't work; he was wide awake and decided he should just get up. He climbed out of bed thinking: day 24,192.

Mark was never rested after the nightmare came calling.

With coffee made, bladder drained, fireplace warming the morning chill, Mark sat down at the laptop to, as he called it, "to peruse the news".

A retired reporter who earned the nickname the "Correspondent of Corpses" because when Mark first started with the newspaper he began writing obituaries but when the veteran crime reporter dropped dead of a heart attack while covering a murder, Mark was promoted to the crime beat and ended up specializing in murders.

Covering the dregs of society for decades didn't seem to outwardly bother Mark as some psychologists might predict, but when he slept, the Demon of Death crept out of his subconscious to haunt his dreams. When he had the nightmare he would awake in a shaking sweat. Mark tried not to awaken Sherry as he got out of bed, grabbed the flashlight he kept in his bedside stand and searched the house. He knew there wasn't anyone or anything in there but he had to do it to convince his subconscious.

Content the house was clear of assassins, butchers, murderers, and pigs, Mark laid down on the couch hoping to fall back to sleep.

Despite the nightmare, Mark was awake at his normal time. He made the coffee, peed and began to peruse the news; Donald Trump insulted another minority group, California is still in a drought, and there was another suicide bomber in the Middle East. As he moved the cursor down the page a headline caught his attention, "Foot Washes up on Canadian Shore."

"Now that sounds interesting," Mark said as he sipped his coffee, opened the article and leaned back to read. The article piqued his interest and he did a Google search for feet washing up on the Canadian Shore. Several pages of entries pop up. Mark selects the oldest entry to get the background information then will work his way to the most current posting. "Hell, why haven't I heard of this before, feet have been washing up in the Vancouver area since 2007."

The idea that 13 human feet have surfaced on beaches all within 125 miles or so of each other caught Mark's attention. His mind with its murderous tendencies after years of documenting death was excitedly taking in all the evidence he could find and writing notes in his notebook.

He clicked on another website, read and made notes. All of the feet were found wearing running shoes of some sort. Most of what remained was just the foot, but at least one had part of the leg attached, some were the right foot and others the left. None of the feet showed signs of violence.

"I wonder if this is some deranged serial killer whose deviance involves removing the feet from the body and throwing them in the ocean," Mark said aloud. "Someone has to be killing these people, but why is it only the feet and not the head, torso or other appendages surfacing? Are they cutting the bodies into pieces and dumping the body parts in the ocean? Are the feet cut off before or after death? Maybe it's some foot worshiping cult that use the feet in a bizarre ritual then disposes of them by throwing them in the ocean. Why are the feet always in gym shoes? Gym shoes, now I'm showing my age. When I grew up we wore P.F. Fliers, Converse and Keds and called them gym shoes or tennis shoes." Mark laughed at himself.

Getting back to the mystery of the feet washing up on the beaches of Vancouver Mark wondered why only the shoes and feet were washing up? If the body was tossed into the ocean to dispose of it you would think the whole body would end up on the beach, unless the sharks are eating the bodies but don't like the taste of running shoes and spit them out.

Mark, with the same enthusiastic interest he had when he was covering a challenging murder as a reporter, read all he could in chronological order, from an article when the first foot appeared, moving towards the most recent discovery. His mind was racing with theories, with thoughts of murder and dismemberment. His enthusiasm came to a crashing halt when he read an article that explained the reason feet were appearing on the beaches of Vancouver.

A scientist explained that after performing DNA tests on the feet and interviewing the relatives of the people whose feet were found, it was determined the feet belonged to mentally ill and distraught and depressed individuals who had committed suicide by jumping off the bridges in the city. Their bodies were carried downstream to the ocean and naturally decomposed, but the feet being encased in the tightly tied shoes slowed decomposition and also sea creatures could not easily feed on them. During decomposition the feet naturally separated from the leg and the shoes being made of buoyant material caused them to float to the surface, ultimately ending up on the beaches.

"Son of a bitch!" Mark exclaimed as Sherry walked down the stairs making her first appearance of the day,

"Well, and a good morning to you too," Sherry said as she and the dog descended the stairs.

Mark turned towards his wife. He was so engrossed in the case of the floating feet he was unaware she and the pooch were awake. "Sorry, not you. It's a murder I was doing some research on. Some feet washed up on ..." Mark said but was cut off by Sherry.

"Save it, I have to pee and the princess probably does too," Sherry said as she shuffled off to the bathroom.

Mark let the dog out, and made a cup of French Vanilla coffee before Sherry reappeared. "Now, what were you saying?"

"Oh, nothing, I thought it was some bizarre serial killer murdering people, cutting them up and throwing their feet in the ocean, but it turned out to be nothing. Well, not exactly nothing, but not as interesting as I thought it might be."

"Sounds disgusting," Sherry said as she scratched the dog, sipped her coffee and checked out the newest posts on Facebook. Mark watched her get settled and thought, "We all have our morning rituals."

Mark was so excited about the possibility of a mystery unfolding in Vancouver that it was a disappointment to learn the truth. He ripped the pages titled "Feet" from his notebook and settled back down at the laptop.

"I guess my overactive imagination got the best of me again," he thought.

He checked The Detroit Free Press main page, not finding anything interesting going on in the Metro Detroit area. He clicked on the Michigan tab and saw an article about a body found in a river in the northern part of lower Michigan. "Well, maybe this will be of interest," Mark hoped.

Outside the cottage, dark had slowly given way to morning's light as Mark took another sip of coffee and began to read the article; the Charlevoix County News was credited with providing the article about a nude female body found by two area fishermen. The body was floating near the bank in a remote section of a river located between Benway and Henley Lakes in Antrim County.

He re-read the article and his old journalistic instincts resurfaced and he asked himself; "I wonder if she was killed there or somewhere else and left there? Was she a local girl or tourist or neither? Heck, maybe she just fell out of a kayak or canoe and drowned with nothing sinister going at all. No, if she fell out of a boat why would she be found nude, unless she was having some well-balanced kayak sex and her partner has yet to surface. I wish the article provided more information."

"This intrigues me," he mumbled as he lifted the coffee cup to his lips. He re-read the article for a third time and decided he would do a search later and see what more had been released about the dead girl.

"Anything else in the news?" Sherry asks.

"No, same old crap, but there is something interesting going on by Charlevoix. A dead girl was found floating in a river."

"You and your murders. I swear you are obsessed with un-natural death. You were probably Jack the Ripper in another life."

"I don't know if she was murdered, probably, but they didn't release much information."

"Mark, you're retired. You don't need to chase murderers around anymore."

Changing the subject Mark said, "Did you know that this is the 24,192th day of my life?"

"What?" she said with a questioning look on her face.

"The other day I was wondering how many mornings I have experienced in my life, and it is 24,192, give or take a few. I didn't take into account leap years. I was going to figure it out exactly, but I got bored."

Sherry sipped her slightly coffee flavored French Vanilla, returned to checking Facebook on the iPad and said, "You're crazy."

Chapter 4

M ark had retired after Thirty-three years of writing for the Detroit Free Press. Murder was his thing. He covered hundreds of murders, mostly in Detroit but also around the state and Great Lakes region. He was still amazed how people could be so cruel and inhumane towards their fellow man.

Through his career, he reported on some of the most horrific crimes to occur; a mother who drowned her three children in the bathtub so her estranged husband wouldn't take them for a weekend visitation, Shelly Brooks, a Detroit serial killer who bludgeoned at least seven prostitutes, and so many drug related shootings that he couldn't remember.

While covering the murder of a woman found beaten to death off U.S. 2 in Michigan's Upper Peninsula, Mark fell in love with the beauty and tranquility of the area. He and Sherry took a vacation in the U.P. and before the week was over they had purchased a small cottage on Dodge Lake, north of Manistique.

They drove north whenever they could to work on the cottage and to relax. After being up to his elbows in death all week, Mark found he could relax and unwind at the cottage. There weren't any police cars to chase to a crime scene, no sirens of an ambulance racing to take a bleeding gunshot victim to a hospital, no deadlines to meet, just an occasional fox running along the shore, the eagle across the lake and ducks nibbling on the seaweed in the shallows. When Mark was at the cottage he was a different person. He was the man Sherry had met in college before all the death changed him.

Although he still suffered the nightmares at the cottage, they weren't as frequent.

When he retired from the Free Press and Sherry from teaching first graders, they sold their house in Dearborn, remodeled the cottage and moved up to the Upper Peninsula. Now Mark only stressed when the fish weren't biting. Murder, which was once his 24/7 vocation, he now followed for amusement. He enjoyed following murders and playing amateur sleuth, theorizing about the crimes based on his decades of chasing the grim reaper.

Just after they moved to the cottage, Mark learned that the National Football team of choice in the U.P. is the Green Bay Packers. Geographically the Upper Peninsula is closer to Lambeau Field in Green Bay than Ford Field in Detroit. If the Packers were playing an opponent at the same time the Lions were playing another, a Lions fan would be hard pressed to find anything but the Packers on any TV in any bar throughout the U.P. The same is true for newspapers. Mark found the Milwaukee Journal is easier to find than a Detroit Free Press. So Mark relies on the online versions of the Detroit papers.

One day when the Internet was out, which seemed to Mark to be an all too frequent occurrence, it threw his schedule into disarray; he couldn't follow his normal morning routine. Mark was so flustered without a morning news source he drove to the small country store not far from the cottage for a newspaper. He bought a Marquette Mining Journal, a Milwaukee Journal, and picked up the free county shopper.

Mark found an article in The Milwaukee Journal so interesting that it consumed his mind for days to come. He read a feature article about one of the most bizarre serial killers in the history of the United States; Eddie Gein.

Gein killed several people and disinterred recently buried bodies in Plainfield, Wisconsin in the 1950's. He was not some ghoulish looking murderer, not a person to avoid out of fear; rather he was a quiet, well liked, mild mannered guy that area folks hired for odd jobs like lawn work and babysitting.

"Sherry, you've got to hear about this guy," Mark said to his wife as he sat reading the article. "When the police paid a visit to the Gein farm they found the headless corpse of a woman hanging from the rafters. The body had been slit open and gutted like a deer and hung over the kitchen sink to drain the blood from the carcass."

"Oh, Mark, shush! You know I don't like hearing about that kind of stuff," Sherry said. She didn't share Mark's fascination with the macabre so he continued to read to himself.

The inventory at Eddie Gein's house of horrors included the kind of ghoulish objects one would only expect to find in a low budget horror movie; lampshades and wastebaskets made of human flesh, tanned and stretched taut over a frame. A bowl found in the kitchen that showed signs of use was made from the top of a human skull and preserved shrunken heads were hanging on a wall as decorations.

A shoebox found in Eddie Gein's bedroom contained souvenirs of his exploits, dried female genitalia. Other items found were a preserved human head, four noses cut from their victims faces, a necklace made of a pair of lips on a string, nine dried human flesh death masks, skulls decorating his bedposts, a heart removed from a corpse and a belt Eddie adorned with nipples from the breasts of the women he killed or corpses he dug up and mutilated.

The most bizarre of Eddie Gein's collection was an object that would inspire the movie "Silence of the Lambs" and Alfred Hitchcock's "Psycho". The investigators found a suit Eddie had fashioned of human flesh. He selected parts of the bodies of the women he killed or dug up, tanned the flesh then sewed together a full body suit of a female, complete with female breasts."

"Sherry, you're not going to believe this guy. He is one very strange cookie."

"Uh-huh," Sherry said continuing to scroll through Facebook postings, not interested in the latest murder that Mark found fascinating.

Once the Internet was back up and running Mark Googled Eddie Gein and read all he could about the unassuming serial killer who killed, disemboweled, skinned, and ate his victims.

~ ~ ~

As he rode the lawn mower around the yard, Mark thought of the strange Eddie Gein and his murders but the thought of the woman found floating in the river downstate kept coming back into his mind. Mark couldn't put his finger on it but he had a nagging feeling that the death of the girl sounded familiar. He stopped the mower, went inside for a glass of iced tea and flipped open the laptop. A quick search provided more information about the floater, a term used in his previous life to describe bodies found in the Detroit River.

Mark found an online article on the Charlevoix County News web site saying the Antrim County Sherriff acknowledged that a body was found and that his office was investigating. He refused to comment on the girl's identification or any other details of the crime. A Charlevoix County News reporter knew one of the guys who discovered the body and the guy, eager for his fifteen minutes of fame, told the reporter all he knew.

The online article said the man and his buddy had launched their 12-foot aluminum boat at the public landing on Benway Lake and were fishing the river south of the lake. They saw something near the west bank and rowed over to it thinking it looked like a suitcase or something. As they got closer the men realized it was a body floating face down. The guy told the reporter how he grabbed an arm rolling the body over revealing the victim was a woman.

The fisherman told the reporter he had seen the girl before, he didn't know her name but he thought she was a waitress at the End Zone, a sports bar in Traverse City. The fisherman said he thought she was strangled because her neck was bruised. "Oh and," he said, there was somethin' pink stuffed in her mouth. Ya know like fabric, like nylon or somethin'."

Mark was reading the article for the third time taking in all details in intense concentration when Sherry yelled from the laundry room, "Mark, your sister called and she and your mother want to come up for a few days in August," as she stuffed sheets into the washer.

"Okay," Mark said as he walked to the kitchen, dumped the ice cubes from his glass into the stainless steel sink and went back out to finish cutting the yard. As he drove around the yard, his mind wasn't on the grass rather it was rolling over what he knew about the dead girl found in the river; a local girl, worked at a bar, possibly strangled, nude, pink fabric stuffed in her mouth, apparently the body had not been in the water very long because the fisherman said he noticed the bruising on her neck. If she had been in the water for a length of time the body would have been bloated and pale and the bruising would not have been so obvious.

"Why does this sound so familiar?" Mark said aloud as he drove the lawn mower in the garage. "I must have covered something similar in the past."

Sherry and Mark went through the day doing all the usual stuff; chores around the cottage, showered and went out to dinner at The Jack Pine Lodge. The parmesan-encrusted whitefish was the special of the day. They ate, had a few drinks and talked to some friends but the thought of the floater occupied Mark's attention. When they returned back to the cottage Mark checked the computer looking for any new information about the girl as Sherry played solitaire on the iPad. Unfortunately he went to bed with no additional information but what he knew kept him thinking. Mark hoped there would be more details online in the morning. He thought for a moment then said to himself, "It will be my 24,193th morning."

Not able to sleep, Mark got out of bed a little after 3:00 AM. Trying not to disturb Sherry or the dog, he grabbed his robe and went downstairs. The case of the dead girl found in an Antrim County river was still on his mind. Sherry would say he was obsessing and he knew she was probably right but he couldn't help himself. At least he didn't wake up in a shaking sweat from a pig nightmare.

"Where is Benway Lake?" he wondered. "I've never heard of it." At 3:26 in the morning Mark grabbed his car keys and walked out in his robe and moccasin slippers to the garage to get a Michigan map from the car. Back inside he unfolded the map on the kitchen counter where he could turn on the ceiling light and it wouldn't bother Sherry or the dog. Mark's index finger found Traverse City and followed M 131 north towards Charlevoix. Finding the gray dashes that outlined Antrim County, he noticed there were several lakes, Torch and Elk lakes were the largest but the map only showed blue shapes of smaller lakes it didn't give their names. Mark couldn't find either Hanley or Benway Lakes.

Disappointed, Mark folded the map on the first try and went to get the laptop. "That'll teach me to go old school, should have checked the computer in the first place." On the kitchen counter he opened the computer. A search quickly turned up a map of Antrim County. He moved the curser around the screen looking for either of the lakes mentioned in the article.

"Son of a Bitch!" Mark said out loud. All of a sudden it hit him, he knew why the girl found floating in the river sounded so familiar; he knew what had been gnawing at him since he first read the article. Mark quickly went to the living room and without a thought of a sleeping Sherry or the dog he flipped on the recessed ceiling lights, brilliantly illuminating the living room and the built-in shelf on the side of the fireplace piled high with books.

Mark silently read the titles as he ran his finger along the spines looking for a specific book.

"Mark! Mark!" Sherry called from the loft. "What are you doing? Are you all right?"

"Oh shit," Mark mumbled, realizing he woke up Sherry. He heard the dog jump out of bed. Mark looked up and saw the little pea-brain peering down the stairs at him with what appeared to be a disgusted look.

"Yeah, sorry, Sher. I'm fine, just looking for a book." He heard the springs of the bed squeak as Sherry turned over and he thought she probably pulled his pillow over her head to shield her eyes from the light.

Mark found what he was looking for and pulled the book from the shelf. He turned off the ceiling lights, went back to the kitchen and sat on a stool at the breakfast bar. Mark opened the book to the index and looked down until he found the chapter he was looking for.

Chapter 5

Sherry walked down the stairs in the morning finding Mark up and typing on the computer. Mark turned his head to look at his wife, "Good morning Hon, I'm sorry about waking you last night but I discovered something about that girl they found in the river."

"What girl?"

"I told you about it yesterday; a female body was found floating in a river downstate, remember? Anyway, something about the whole thing sounded familiar and I couldn't sleep so I got up and was looking for the river where she was found. The article said the guys who discovered her launched their boat at the public launch ramp on Benway Lake and found her in the river south of the lake. The river south of Benway Lake is the Green River!" Mark said excitedly.

Sherry looked at her husband, smiled and said "Okay Honey," and shuffled off to the bathroom with the dog following. She had seen him this way before. She called it his "Eureka Mood", the excitement he gets when things come together.

When she returned to her chair next to the fireplace with her cup of coffee flavored French Vanilla, Mark said, "You have to listen to this, it's amazing, really fantastic. Like I told you the girl's body was found floating in the Green River. It's just a little river between two small lakes by Charlevoix."

Sherry looked at her husband while sipping her drink. She nodded her head trying to look interested. She enjoyed seeing him so excited. She hadn't seen him this animated since before he retired.

"And the guy who found her said there was a pink fabric stuffed in her mouth. I knew it all sounded familiar but couldn't figure out why and then it hit me," he said smacking his palm against his forehead. "I read about a killing that sounded a lot like this. It was driving me crazy trying to remember where I had heard of it before. Then last night it hit me, it was in the book you bought me for my birthday. Remember the one about serial killers called *Rampage*?"

"Oh yeah, that book," Sherry said, "the *Rampage* book."

"It's a book by," Mark turns the book to look at the cover, "Wayne Louis Kadar, an author who lives in Michigan and he writes true crime and regional books about the Great Lakes area."

Mark opened the book to the page he had bookmarked with a blue sticky note. He began to read the text he had highlighted with a yellow marker:

"On July 15, the body of Bonnie Coffield, a runaway, was found floating in the river. She was nude with her panties sadistically stuffed in her mouth."

Mark looked up from the book at Sherry. "Do you see it? A naked girl was found floating in the GREEN River in Michigan," he said emphasizing Green, "and she had a pink fabric stuffed in her mouth, and in the *Rampage* book a naked girl was found floating in the GREEN River in Washington State with her panties stuffed in her mouth. Now that can't be a coincidence. That was an excerpt from the chapter about the GREEN River Killer in Washington State. I think there is something more to the murder of the

Michigan girl. I think someone is copying Gary Ridgway, the Green River Killer!"

Sherry asked, "Do people often copy other killers?"

Mark thought for a moment and said, "I don't know." He hadn't thought about that.

Chapter 6

The sky was dark and gray. Thunder interrupted the quiet and lightening flashed in the distance as rain drops formed rings on the surface of the lake. For two days Mark and Sherry were forced to stay inside. Sherry caught up with friends on Facebook, talked with their daughter in Frankenmuth, read one of her trashy novels, played Solitaire and Scrabble on the iPad and napped. Mark re-read the Green River Killer chapter of the serial killer book, highlighting important text and writing in a notebook. When he wasn't reading or writing, he was flipping pages of the notebook over the metal spiral along the top, re-reading his notes.

The stormy weather held life's obligations at bay; no lawn to cut, no beach to rake, no car to wash and allowed Mark to concentrate on the murdered girl found in Michigan's Green River and the killings of Gary Ridgway. Ridgway was dubbed the Green River Killer for dumping the bodies of his first five victims either in or near the Green River in Washington State. Mark studied the Green River chapter in the *Rampage* book, and studied articles online from the Charlevoix County News. There wasn't a lot; the police were not releasing much information but Mark found that a reporter from the Traverse City Record-Eagle was doing some investigative work on her own and wrote an article about her findings.

From the article Mark learned the victim's name was Bonnie Winslow, she was 23-years old and was originally from Elk Rapids. She was working at the End Zone the night she disappeared and was found the following day.

Mark decided he would give the reporter a call and flipped a few pages of his notebook to the first page and wrote, "Karrie Stanford - Record-Eagle –Call". Then he jotted down a few questions he would ask her, just like he did when he was writing for the Free Press.

With a quick Google search Mark found the phone number for the Traverse City Record-Eagle and even an extension and email address for Karrie Stanford. He punched the number into his phone and when asked for an extension he pressed #305. Expecting to get Ms. Stanford's voice mail he mentally prepared a message but was surprised when a voice answered, "Stanford."

Mark thought, it's her not a machine. "Hi Ms. Stanford, this is Mark Daniels I work with the Detroit Free Press."

Mark thought to himself, "I'm not lying, last month I did write a feature article about life in the Upper Peninsula and if there was a minor story in the UP my old editor would call me rather than go through the expense of sending a reporter up from Detroit. No, I'm not lying, exaggerating, maybe."

"Hello Mr. Daniels, how can I help you?" the young sounding voice asked.

Mark said, "I have been reading your articles on the girl found floating in a river there. I was wondering if you would mind a couple questions?"

Karrie answered, "Sure, how can I help the Free Press?"

Mark ignored the fact that she sounded as though she thought he was a staff reporter with the Free Press, looked down at his notebook and asked his first question.

"What can you tell me about the victim?"

Karrie answered, "Well she is a local girl, raised in Elk Rapids up north of here. Quit high school in her junior year and ran off to Chicago with her dirtbag boyfriend.

26

When he was busted for dealing drugs and sent to Joliet she moved back north and got a job at the End Zone."

"Does she have a record?" Mark asked.

"Ah, yeah, let me find it." Mark could hear her shuffling through papers. "Here it is. While she was in Chicago she was busted on a prostitution charge. Her boyfriend turned her out and sold drugs. Nice guy huh? My editor didn't want me to include any of that."

"Do you think she was turning tricks in Traverse City?" Mark asked.

"Can't say for sure, but a cop I know said they suspected she was meeting guys in the End Zone parking lot to... ah...supplement her income."

Mark asked, "Was she "supplementing" with someone that night?"

"I talked to the bar manager and the bartender that was working the night she disappeared and they said they didn't suspect she was doing anything other than pushing drinks. I think they are covering their asses, trying to keep the name of the bar out of the news. Not quite the kind of publicity they want."

Mark looked over the questions penciled in his notebook. "Do you know a cause of death?"

"Nope, not yet. The coroner still has the body and hasn't announced anything yet. As soon as we hear it will be in the newspaper and in our online edition too," Karrie answered.

"What interest does the Free Press have in this?" she asked.

Mark was caught off guard with the question and quickly thought of an answer, "Oh just checking it out. I thought it may have some connection with another case, but probably not."

"By the way Mr. Daniels, I liked that piece you wrote on John Norman Collins."

"Oh thank you," Mark said, amazed that the girl would have known about his feature; *John Norman Collins-20 Years Later*" and knew it was he who wrote it. "I'm honored you remember it. That was a few years back."

"I wrote a report on it in one of my journalism classes. I remembered my mom talking a lot about John Norman Collins and how it scared her and her friends when they were in college at Eastern Michigan. I came across your article and decided to write about it. And I got an A on the assignment," Karrie proudly said.

Getting back to the subject, Karrie said, "This murder has everyone around here talking. One of the veteran reporters who has been working for the paper since the dinosaurs roamed says the Bonnie Winslow murder is drawing about as much attention as the Good Hart murders did back in 1968."

"Mr. Daniels, I have to go, I have to interview a guy whose dog had a litter of 17 puppies. I'm sure you had some of those "hard news" stories in your career too, but call me anytime and I've got your number here on my caller ID so I can call you if anything new comes up with our girl. It was a pleasure talking with you."

"Karrie, thank you for the information, you've been very helpful. And it was my pleasure talking with you," Mark said.

It was almost five o'clock and Mark walked to the kitchen for a drink. He took the vodka down off the shelf, poured some in a glass, capped the bottle and returned it to the shelf. As he was reaching in the refrigerator for the bloody Mary mix Sherry asked snidely, "Isn't it a little early for a drink?"

Mark explained as he poured the red concoction into his glass, "I have a lot of thinking to do and this will either help me focus or help me nap." Then he noticed a half full glass of wine on the counter behind Sherry. Mark smiled and asked, "And who is questioning me about starting early?"

Chapter 7

Mark was mentally reviewing his conversation with Karrie, and thought about the Good Hart murder she had referred to. Mark vaguely remembered the killing of the family at their cottage on the shore of Lake Michigan. It occurred during his freshman year and before he had an interest in murder.

Mark did a Google search for Good Hart, Michigan. Several listings appeared ranging from the Good Hart Chamber of Commerce, a map showing the location of Good Hart north of Harbor Springs and south of Cross Village, a listing for the Good Hart General Store, and a listing entitled, Good Hart Murders. Mark moved his cursor to that one and clicked.

He read an article about the Robison family; father Richard, the owner of a Detroit area advertising company, his wife Shirley and their four children; Ritchie, 19, Gary, 17, Randy, 12 and Susan, 8. The entire family was gunned down in their cottage, victims of a murderer.

One day a neighbor noticed a foul odor coming from the direction of the Robison cottage and since she had not seen the family for a while and figured they were gone, she called the family's caretaker to report that an animal must have gotten into the crawl space and died.

The caretaker arrived at the cottage, used his key to open the door and was met with a burst of foul smelling hot air and a swarm of flies. The dead bodies of the six Robison family members lay for 27 days before the caretaker entered. The murderer turned the cottage furnace to high and from the temperature in the cabin and the length of time they laid unnoticed. The bodies were severely decomposed and covered with flies and maggots.

Sheriff's deputies wearing breathing respirators entered the cabin to discover Mrs. Robison's bloated and maggot covered body lying on the living room floor. She had been shot, covered with a blanket and posed with her knees raised and parted giving the impression she had been sexually assaulted. Mr. Robison's dead body was placed over the furnace floor register to hasten the decomposition. Twelve-year-old Randy was killed and placed on top of his father and covered with a blanket. Susan, the couple's only daughter was left near her father and brother. The other two older boys were found lying on the floor in the back bedroom apparently where they had been shot and dropped.

The investigation was led by the Michigan State Police. The police investigated every tip they received. There was talk that some bizarre cult was involved in the murders, but it proved to be just a rumor. One theory was that the caretaker murdered the family because of some misunderstanding but that also proved to be untrue. Another thought was that since the older son was attending Eastern Michigan University at the same time as John Norman Collins (the Michigan Co-Ed Killer), possibly their paths crossed and maybe Collins for some reason killed the family. None of the theories or rumors proved credible; however, the investigation began to focus on Richard Robison's business partner Joseph Scolaro.

The police found that it appeared Scolaro had been embezzling from the advertising company the two men owned and might have killed Richard and his family when he was found out. Scolaro said he was innocent and while he did not have an iron clad alibi, he claimed he couldn't possibly have left work, driven from the Detroit area to

Good Hart, murdered the family and returned to Detroit by the time his wife reported seeing him the next day.

The investigation ran into a lot of dead ends but it also did not develop any new credible suspects. It was agreed that Richard Robison's business partner, Joseph Scolaro was the primary suspect. On March 8, 1973, almost five years after the murders of the Robison family in their cottage in Good Hart, Joseph Scolaro killed himself with a single gunshot to the head. In his suicide note he said he professed his innocence by claiming he was a lot of things but he was not a murderer.

The murder of the Robison family in rural North West Michigan was never solved and remains one of Michigan's most notorious cold cases.

Mark scrolled down looking at the bibliography for the article and noticed a book entitled, *Great Lakes Cold Case Files; Unsolved Murders of the Great Lakes Region* by Wayne Louis Kadar, the same author who wrote the *Rampage* book. He wrote the title and author's name down in his notebook saying, "I'm going to have to get this book."

Chapter 8

Day 24,200 in the life of Mark Daniels started as so many others had, awake at 5:17, coffee, pee, and peruse the news. He was searching for more information about the murdered girl in Antrim County but found it was as if she was yesterday's news and nothing new was reported. Karrie had an article but it was mostly just a summary of her previous articles, nothing he didn't already know.

Mark's phone beeped indicating a text and found information from Karrie Stanford stating that the coroner determined that Bonnie Winslow's cause of death was manual asphyxiation.

It was the only new bit of evidence he had found on the death of the girl in the Green River since he talked to Karrie five days ago. But it was an important piece of the puzzle. Manual asphyxiation means the killer used his hands to strangle the full time waitress and part time prostitute.

Mark flipped the pages of his notebook until he found what he was looking for, pencil lines drawn the length of the page forming three columns. At the top of the first column he had written "Known Facts", the second column was labeled Washington, the third Michigan. The last entry on the bottom of the first column read; "Cause of Death". To the right in the Washington column he had written "Strangulation" and now under the Michigan column he wrote "Strangulation".

Mark looked at the columns and the similarities between the murders that took place in Washington state and the murder of Bonnie Winslow in Michigan; body found floating in river, river's name – Green, victim was nude, victim was a known prostitute, panties stuffed in victim's mouth, cause of death – strangulation. No, definitely too many similarities for it to be a coincidence.

Mark pondered what he should do with his findings, should he notify the Antrim County Sherriff's department? Should he call Karrie Stanford at the Traverse City Record-Eagle? Should he call the FBI? Should he just mind his own business and keep quiet. When he asked Sherry her opinion, she reminded him that he was retired and no longer had to deal in death.

Mark went through his day, building shelves in the garage and raking the beach, but his thoughts never drifted far from the death of the 23-year old waitress from the End Zone who was probably just trying to make ends meet by...making ends meet. He smiled at his own joke. But this time she apparently had met the wrong man and he ended up killing her.

A little after 3:00 Mark settled down on the couch, flipped open the laptop and Googled Antrim County Sheriff for the phone number. He opened his notebook to the page with the three columns of similarities and punched the phone number in his cell.

He asked to talk to the person investigating the death of the girl found floating in the river. Mark was transferred to the voice mail of Detective Semp. Mark wrote the name in his notebook then left a message; "I'm Mark Daniels with the Detroit Free Press and I would like to talk to you about the murder of Bonnie Winslow." He left his phone number and recorded the date and time he called the detective in his notebook.

The fact that he might be withholding evidence in the death of a young woman weighed on him and Mark felt better now that he called the Sheriff's department. Now he just had to wait for a call back.

Sherry had overheard Mark talking on the phone and said, "You couldn't just leave it alone could you?"

"No, it would drive me crazy if I didn't tell the authorities of the information I uncovered," Mark said.

Sherry handed Mark a glass and sat down in her favorite chair, the La-Z-Boy next to the fireplace. Mark tasted the drink, and looked at his wife, "There's rum in this Coke. It's a little early isn't it?"

"Yeah, but you've been stressing over this murder and I thought you needed to relax. Mark, why did you tell the police that you were from the Detroit Free Press?" Sherry asked.

"Well, I figured it may give more credence to my theory when they hear the name of a well-respected newspaper."

Sherry said, "Or they may take offense to a big city newspaper butting into a local investigation. What if they call the paper and find out you don't work there anymore?"

"Yeah, maybe. I didn't think of it that way," Mark said, taking a sip of the drink and staring out the wall of glass noticing the eagle soaring high above the far side of the lake and thinking maybe he should call the deputy back tomorrow.

That evening as they sat by the fireplace with Eric Clapton playing the slow version of *Layla* on Pandora, Sherry was playing Scrabble on the iPad and the iPad was winning. Mark picked up the *Rampage* book off the coffee table where it sat since the night he made the discovery that the Washington State Green River murders were similar to the Antrim County Green River murder. Starting from the first chapter he read and scribbled in his notebook. "I need to find a new book to read and get away from all the death," he thought.

Chapter 9

Mark had a nightmare that night. In the dream, a man and a friend in their late twenties were drinking and shooting pool in a rural northern Michigan bar. He could see the bar, the tables, the knotty pine paneling and chairs and the people talking, drinking and having fun, but in the dream Mark was viewing the scene through the glass eyes of a 10-point buck stuffed and hanging on the stone chimney of the fireplace above the mantel.

Through the eyes of the deer high above the bar, he could see it was a busy night. The locals that were there almost every night were sitting on their stools. The Duvall brothers, Ray and Don, were pounding down beers and Mark could see that Barbara was flirting with a guy who worked at the mill. Filling the bar were men and a few women who journeyed north to hunt the elusive white tail deer. They were dressed in flannel shirts, sweatshirts and jeans, many still in hunter's orange and they stuck out like a sore thumb to the locals.

The two guys shooting pool were drunk and loud. They weren't obnoxious or rude, just a couple of guys away from home for a few days having fun and drinking too much. The taller of the two took aim on the cue ball. If he judged the angle correctly, the cue ball would strike the eight ball, the black ball would rebound off the far cushion and roll the length of the green felt covered table and drop in the left end pocket, winning the game.

He slowly drew back his cue stick, shoved it forward. The end of the stick struck the cue ball, the white ball struck the black ball, the black ball traveled to the cushion, bounced off and began its trajectory towards the other end of the table, but in his present state of inebriation, he misjudged the angle. The eight ball missed the pocket and bounced off the end cushion and took aim for the left side pocket. He yelled, "No! You son of a bitch, no!"

Heads in the bar turned, to see what the commotion was about, many anticipating a fight which could turn into a bar clearing brawl; entertainment for the night.

The eight ball slowly rolled towards the side pocket and dropped in with the sound of hard plastic on wood and the shooter shouted to his buddy, louder than necessary, "Fuck!"

Ray Duvall looked up at the two men up north to kill their deer, glared at the pool players in disgust and hatred and mumbled, "Fuckin assholes."

Mark watched from his perch above the fireplace mantel, Barbara and her new friend left the bar together, Ray and his brother Don, tired of the arrogant hunters who invaded their bar, hunted their deer and picked up the local women, left the bar. The two inebriated hunters who were shooting pool sat down at a table to finish their beers.

The two guys, David Tyll and Brian Ognjan, friends for decades, enjoyed their annual hunting trip north. They got away from home for a few days, away from the responsibilities of life. Once out of the watchful eyes of wives, girlfriends and family, they ate what they wanted and drank too much, like many of the hunters that took to the woods of northern Michigan during deer season.

With bottles empty, the two guys, heavily intoxicated, pushed away from the table and rose unsteadily to leave. Mark yelled to them, "No, don't go outside!" but the words didn't come out of the deer's mouth. "No! They're waiting for you!" But the guys couldn't hear Mark's warning, they walked out of the bar. They didn't know the Duvall brothers were waiting outside with baseball bats.

In a panic, Mark sat up in his bed and shouted, "Don't leave!" waking himself, Sherry and the dog.

"Mark, it's just a dream, it was just a dream," Sherry said, rubbing Mark's clammy back.

Mark looked around the loft and realizing he wasn't in the bar said, "Sorry, it was the nightmare again." He got out of bed and said. "Go back to sleep, Hon."

Chapter 10

The next morning Mark was not rested. He never was after death paid him a nocturnal visit, but he got up at his regular time and followed his normal routine. As a diversion from the murder case that was consuming his time, Mark began reading David Maraniss's book "Once in a Great City... A Detroit Story." The book had been highly recommended to him from a friend who worked at the Free Press. He had said, "Mark, you have to read this book. It's all about the early 1960's and what made Detroit great; Ford, Chrysler, General Motors, Motown, J.L. Hudson's but it also relates what ultimately led to the city's downfall."

Sherry walked downstairs with the dog lazily following and asked, "Mark, are you okay?"

Mark looked at his bride and said, "Yeah, just a dream," trying to dismiss the embarrassing fragility that haunted his nights.

"Was it the pigs again?"

Mark shook his head saying, "Nope, no pigs this time."

While waiting for the Antrim County Sheriff's office to call him back, Mark divided his time between yard work, fishing, the serial killer book and reading the Maraniss book. But nothing seemed to keep him from thinking about Bonnie Winslow. What were her last words? What was her final thought? Did she scream? Did she know her killer? Questions he thought would probably never be answered.

He sat in the aluminum fishing boat drifting on the lake, a rod in his hand and the murdered girl on his mind.

Mark wondered why he didn't get a call back from the Sheriff's investigator. "It's been four days since I called. You would think they would welcome a tip on the murder."

"Maybe they have a suspect in custody and are busy building a case and don't need my input or maybe they think I'm just some crackpot calling from a 906 area code in the Upper Peninsula," Mark thought as he mindlessly watched the red and white bobber floating on the surface of the tranquil lake. "Hell, maybe I am just a crackpot with an overactive imagination from a history full of death," he mumbled aloud.

~ ~ ~

Mark put his book down and got up from the recliner. He raised his empty glass to his wife, a nonverbal question asking if she wanted a refill. She raised hers showing she still had half of a glass of red wine. Mark walked to the kitchen and he mused about since they had been married for so long and knew each other so well they didn't need to rely on talking; they read each other's minds.

Mark was pouring the rum into his glass when he was startled by his cell phone ringing. He quickly walked to the living room wondering who would be calling him in the evening. "Hello?"

"Mr. Daniels?" the voice on the other end of the line asked.

"Yes, this is Mark Daniels."

"Mr. Daniels, this is Detective Semp from the Antrim County Sheriff's department. You called a couple of days ago saying you had some information about a case we are working on," the detective.

Mark looked at Sherry, pointed to the phone and shook his head up and down. She, in her nonverbal way smiled and mouthed "Good." She knew Mark had been waiting for this call for days.

"Well, I am retired from the Detroit Free Press. I was a crime reporter for about thirty years and now I write feature stories for them," Sherry heard Mark explaining.

"I was doing some research into the death of Bonnie Winslow and realized that her death was remarkably similar to a murder that occurred in Washington State." Sherry watched as Mark listened to the detective.

"In 1982," Mark answered a question.

"Gary Ridgway strangled a prostitute and dumped her nude body in the Green River. She was found with her panties stuffed in her mouth, and from what I have discovered that is the same as the murdered girl that was found in Antrim County."

"Ah ha, ah ha," Mark said. "But look at the similarities, both were found in a Green River, both nude, both found with..."

Mark listened as the detective interrupted him saying, "Thank you Mr. Daniels for your insights. I'll pass the information along to the task force and get back to you if we need any additional details." Then he hung up.

Mark pushed the call end button and looked at Sherry, "I got the brush off." He knew the brush off. He had given it often through his years as a reporter. Whenever the newspaper offered a reward for information leading to an arrest in a crime the crackpots came out of the woodwork with off the wall tips trying to claim the money. It was the first time Mark was on the receiving end and it hurt. He went back to finish making his drink, changing it to a double.

Sitting back down, he grabbed the serial killer book he had been reading and left on the arm of his chair. He closed it and tossed it to the coffee table. He was done with the book.

~ ~ ~

For the next few days Mark didn't think about the murder of Bonnie Winslow; he didn't want to think of it. The detective made him feel like some meddling idiot, made him feel like an old man that life was passing by, like his opinion no longer mattered. Mark cast a line in the lake from the dock. The bobber landed with a little splash and he slowly wound the reel taking in line, no nibbles. "Looks like the fish don't want to pay attention to me anymore either."

Sherry watched Mark slip into depression. He had spent a lot of time researching the similarities of the murders, and developing a theory, and the deputy shot down his hypothesis without even hearing him out. She urged him to continue to follow the murder and look for more similarities but he said, "Naw, I'm done with it."

Chapter 11

After days of sulking around and not finding any enjoyment in life Mark knew he had to change his attitude. The small passions in his life didn't hold his attention any longer; fishing, reading, murders, even sex. He felt the fish were avoiding him, he didn't want to read about serial killers and he found everything else boring. He hadn't checked newspaper websites for new murders and he even turned down Sherry when she lowered the lights, cuddled up next to him on the couch in front of the fireplace, pressed her body against his, kissed him and rubbed his thigh. He knew he was depressed because he never turned down sex when Sherry initiated it.

But, he was embarrassed and hurt by the detective. In his prime Mark was an expert on Michigan murders. There were times law enforcement reached out to him for advice, but now the Antrim County detective made him feel like just another tipster to be politely listened to and dismissed. Mark felt insignificant.

He laid his head on his pillow that night and was determined he had to find his way out of the funk. He decided he had to move on past the embarrassment of his brush off by the Antrim County detective.

The detective was probably right in dismissing him, Mark thought. What could a murder committed thirty years earlier, thousands of miles away possibly have to do with a dead girl found in Antrim County, Michigan? It was probably just a theory developed in his overactive imagination fueled by years of chasing the grim reaper.

Besides, he thought, I don't want to turn down Sherry again.

Mark woke up and followed his normal morning routine but without the same enthusiasm of the past.

He decided if he was to dig his way out of the depression he had fallen into he had to make some changes in his life. He wasn't going to follow the Bonnie Winslow case anymore. He had let his hobby become an obsession. He was still going to pursue his hobby of following murder but would follow death from a distance.

When he retired, Mark thought about writing a book about the murders he covered for the newspaper. Most of the research he had done over the years while working for the Free Press was in file boxes on shelves in the garage. "Maybe I should write a book, maybe a novel, a mystery or maybe true crime," Mark thought. "Lord knows I've got enough background in the subject, and I've been writing professionally for decades."

The next day Sherry didn't say anything but she could see Mark was getting better; he wasn't moping around. He even came up behind Sherry standing at the kitchen counter, reached around her and cupped her breasts through the robe saying, "I'm sorry about last night, give me a chance to make it up to you tonight," then kissed the back of her neck.

That evening, buoyed with two inches of whisky over ice, Mark forced himself back into his old routine. He checked the Detroit News for anything of interest; a shooting on Detroit's east side, the police thought was gang related and a man was found floating in the Detroit River off River Rouge. The floater, the article suggested, could be the body of a man missing since he jumped from the Ambassador Bridge a week before.

Mark checked the Chicago Tribune website finding it was a busy weekend in the windy city. Most of the crime reported sounded to be gang or drug related, probably both, but nothing caught his interest. Out of boredom Mark checked USA Today. He read a few articles but most were about the presidential election and politics just wasn't his thing. One article caught his attention; a nurse working at a Veterans hospital was arrested for suspicion of murdering several patients in her care by injecting epinephrine, an untraceable heart stimulant, into their IV bags. The nurse was shocked at the accusations and proclaimed her innocence. He wrote the details of the murdering nurse in his notebook just in case he wanted to check it out later.

Mark decided to do a search for unsolved murders in the Midwest, thinking how research was so much easier now than when he first started working for the Free Press. Then he would spend hours in a library looking over paper copies of old newspapers for some tidbit of information, or he would call law enforcement agencies across the nation hoping they would give him material he could use. But now with the Internet, a few taps on the keyboard and there was a wealth of knowledge available to anyone.

His search turned up a lot of websites with information pertaining to recent murders in the Midwest. He selected an FBI site that contained information cleared for the public and clicked on it. From a dropdown box he selected Michigan and began reading about unsolved murders in the state. He scribbled in his notebook under the heading, "Book Notes." He did the same for Minnesota and Wisconsin. Ohio had only a few recent murders and they were of no interest. The Illinois page contained many more citations of unsolved murders and he took notes. Mark made a drink before he ventured out of the Great Lakes region and onto the Missouri page.

He handed Sherry a glass of wine, her usual evening libation. She said, "Thanks. And Mark, welcome back."

Then she winked at him, happy to see he was back to himself.

Mark sat back down and opened the Missouri page. There were only eight entries, each providing a listing of the pertinent data; name if known, location, date missing, date found, male/female, and age. They also provided a brief summary paragraph about the murder, such as how the victim was killed and other material that might help the public in solving the crime. A phone number was provided for the Missouri Crime Hotline for people to call with tips.

Before he had a chance to read the fifth case summary, Sherry pushed the laptop closed and said, "Come on, time for bed."

Chapter 12

Mark slept well, he usually did after sex, not even waking up to pee in the middle of the night, but at 5:17 he was awake and walking down the stairs. He thought, "This is day 24 thousand..." But he couldn't remember and he realized he no longer really cared either.

He started the fireplace to chase the morning chill, made coffee, peed and settled down on the couch with the computer on his lap. Following his usual routine he checked the Detroit Free Press and USA Today and found something of interest in both. What he read wasn't about murders, rather an article about the latest lawsuit filed against the State of Michigan trying to stop the construction of a second bridge across the Detroit River and an editorial about the proposed pipeline to transport crude oil down from Canada. There was also an editorial written by a person in the Upper Peninsula about the damage the wolves were doing to the farming and hunting community in the U.P. and the need for a wolf-hunting season. The wolves group together in packs and have been killing deer, farm animals and pets.

Sherry walked down the stairs earlier than usual, in fact a look at the clock and Mark realized it was much earlier. He opened the front door, peered out for wildlife that looked hungry enough to eat Sherry's little hairball, then let it out.

By the time the dog came in from her morning pee, Sherry appeared from hers. "Hi Sweetie," she said bending down to give Mark a kiss on the forehead as she walked to her chair next to the fireplace. "Did you sleep well?"

Mark winked at his wife, and said, "I slept great. How about you?"

Sherry took a sip of the French vanilla coffee Mark had prepared for her, winked at her husband and said, "I slept fantastic!"

As the sun climbed in the east and the temperature warmed, Mark decided he would take the aluminum boat out and try to entice dinner to bite his hook.

The fish didn't ignore Mark this time; the big ones did but Mark's confidence got a boost by catching several little ones. Nothing big enough to keep but it was fun catching them and tossing them back in to grow to a legal size.

Mark and Sherry didn't dine on fresh perch that evening, rather it was Hamburger Helper stroganoff that graced their plates. They washed the dishes together, he washed and she dried and put them away.

Mark poured two glasses of wine and by the light of the fireplace Sherry cuddled up next to Mark on the couch. They watched the setting sun, its reflection rippling on the lake, two crows noisily arguing over something and the pair of swan that had taken up residence on the lake.

"I'm thinking of writing a book," Mark said staring out the window.

Sherry looked at Mark and said, "Good, you should. Put your experience to a good use. What kind of book, a mystery?"

"I don't know yet. I'm thinking a novel. I've been taking notes but I have to figure out how it will flow. I don't have it all worked out yet, but you my pretty lady will be the first to know," he said as he picked up her glass of wine from the coffee table and handed it to her.

They sat sipping their wine, enjoying being close, enjoying natures pallet painting the sky until the obnoxious ring tone of Sherry's cell phone interrupted the romantic setting.

"It's Mickie!" Sherry said.

Mark reached for the laptop as Sherry got up and settled in her recliner, the phone to her ear. He opened the computer and went to the Detroit News site and read a few articles then opened the USA Today site looking for anything new about the nurse who was accused of killing her patients, but there wasn't anything other than the article he found earlier.

Mark moved the cursor to his favorite's page and clicked on the site he had saved last night; FBI Open Investigations. He quickly reviewed the Great Lake states to see if anything new had been added then opened to the Missouri page.

Mark couldn't remember what he had read the night before when Sherry seduced him, so he skimmed through the entries starting at the top, but as he read the fifth posting he loudly exclaimed, "Son of a Bitch!"

"Mark!" Sherry said sternly. He forgot that she was on the phone talking to their daughter.

Mark said, "Oh, sorry, but I just found something interesting. Tell Mickie I apologize, but I just found a really cool murder, maybe something I can use in the book."

Sherry said in the receiver, "Oh it's just your dad and one of his murders."

The fifth listing on the website was a murder of an 18-year old man and his 17-year old girlfriend that occurred over a month and half ago. The young couple was parked at a local "lover's lane" near Gravois Mills, Missouri. They were locked in a romantic embrace when suddenly the passenger side window of the car exploded in a thousand shards of glass as three shots were fired from outside the car. The girl was killed instantly by a bullet to the head and the boy lived just a few hours more.

Mark had the date of the shooting, the town where it occurred and the names of the kids killed, so he did a search for a Gravois Mills newspaper website and found the Lake Sun Leader, who billed themselves a daily for the Lake of the Ozarks area. That turned up more information about the case. The boy, Bart Stewart was a freshman at Lincoln University home for the weekend to visit his girlfriend, Debbie Daugherty, a senior at the high school. The couple had gone to the Cinema 5 in Gravois Mills and on the way home they turned off Stoker Road onto a deserted two track for a little alone time.

Although mortally wounded, Bart showed embarrassment when he told the police that the windows were fogged up and didn't see anyone outside the car before the shots were fired. He didn't know there was anyone around until the windows burst into fragments. The kids didn't seem to have any enemies; in fact they were well liked. They came from good families and were active members in the Gravois Mills United Methodist Church. The police had no suspects and no evidence. It appeared to be a completely random shooting and after 47 days of investigating the police had nothing more than when they started. The article listed the contact information for Detectives Shirk and Willard, the lead investigators.

"What is your problem?" Sherry asked her husband once she was off the phone. "Yelling profanities like some mad man."

"I found a murder in Missouri that is interesting," Mark said not looking up from the screen. "It's a couple of kids who were parking and someone shot out the window, killing both kids."

"That's terrible," Sherry said preparing to challenge the iPad to a game of Scrabble.

Mark searched for all he could on the murder of the two Missouri teenagers and scribbled in his notebook. He had several pages of notes before it was time to let the dog out and climb the stairs to the bedroom loft.

As he lay next to a snoring Sherry and almost as loud snoring dog, Mark thought about the Missouri kids. He wondered if the police had a suspect yet, wondered if there had been other killings like it. He wondered if there was a jealous ex-boyfriend or girlfriend, or if they were involved in the drug scene and it was retribution for a deal gone bad? He had so many questions and so few answers. He thought maybe he could base a fictional book on the case; a book about a psychotic killer who stalked young lovers murdering unsuspecting kids in parked cars.

Chapter 13

A cold front was tracking across Minnesota taking aim at the Upper Peninsula and Mark and Sherry decided it was a good day to stay in with the fireplace providing ambiance and heat as they watched the winds of the front blow in from the west.

Mark was renewed, his excitement back, his energy returned. Sherry smiled, she was happy he bounced back so quickly this time. She remembered the time after the pig murders when the nightmares started and Mark was depressed and withdrawn for weeks but refused to seek professional help. But now he had a purpose, he was going to write a book and use the years and years of experience and knowledge he possessed as a basis for a book about murders.

Sherry curled up on her recliner with the dog in her lap and opened a Sudoku book while Mark sat on the couch with the laptop on the coffee table. Sherry watched as Mark stared out the glass wall facing the lake deep in thought. She said, "Hellooo. Mark, where are you?"

Mark's concentration disrupted, he turned to his wife saying, "Oh, sorry, did you say something?"

"You were staring out the windows like you were lost in a dream."

"I was thinking about the book I may write. You know stuff like; should it be factual or fictional or a fictional book based on fact. Should it be a mystery, thriller, horror, or a good old blood and guts gory story?"

"And, what did you decide?" Sherry asked.

"I haven't made up my mind yet, probably a mystery, but I want to do more research to make up my mind."

"Whatever you decide I am sure the book will be a best seller," Sherry said with the confidence of a wife.

"I may base the story on the murders I have been following, you know the girl in the river down by Charlevoix or the kids murdered in Missouri. But I'm sure there are more sensational murders out there I haven't found yet that I can use as a basis.

"Well, if you write some nasty blood and guts horror book I probably won't read it," Sherry said with a look of disgust on her face.

"I really don't know yet what I'm going to do. I'm in the early stages and I'm sure it will evolve as I work my way through it."

Mark looked at the laptop and took a sip of his coffee, which had cooled while he was deep in thought then picked up his notebook. "There was that nurse that was killing patients, where was that?"

"What?" Sherry asked.

"Oh, nothing. I didn't realize I was talking out loud."

Mark and Sherry, warmed by the fire, watched the storm front slide in with thunder and lightning and torrential downpours. She did Sudoku, and played Scrabble and Mark burned up gigabytes on the computer searching for interesting crimes that he could use as a premise for his book. There was a man in Texas who was barricaded in his house holding his mother and sister as hostages and threatening to kill them if the Rangers didn't leave him alone.

A woman and her child were murdered in Montana. The dead woman, a widow, had met the man on an online dating service. He didn't turn out to be her Mr. Right, he turned out to be her Mr. Wrong... her executioner. He killed her and buried her in the dirt floor of the basement then told the neighbors the woman and child had gone on vacation and he was there to housesit while they were away. The neighbors called the police but the man left before they arrived.

It was almost five o'clock when there was a break in the rain and Sherry let the dog out. "I never saw the princess poop and pee so quickly," Sherry said. "Ready for a cocktail?" she asked Mark.

"I'll get them," Mark said putting the laptop on the coffee table and rubbing his eyes while he stretched. "I could use a break from the computer. I feel like a Manhattan, want one?"

Sherry thought for a minute and said, "Sure, we haven't had one of those is a long time."

The whisky, sweet vermouth and a dash of bitters were mixed over ice. Mark put two cherries on a plastic sword in Sherry's glass, and an olive in his. He knew an olive wasn't the traditional garnish for a Manhattan but he didn't like cherries but he loved olives.

"What have you been looking at on the computer," Sherry asked.

"Oh, you know me, it was just some murder stuff."

"You are the only guy I know who can spend hours on end on the computer and not be watching pornography," Sherry said.

"Who said I didn't click on some porn sites and watch a little, strictly for research of course?" He looked her over with a mischievous look from the top of her head to her slipper covered feet with strategic pauses at key parts of her anatomy.

"Jeez! Are you ever satisfied?" she asked in mock distain.

"Honey, the day I'm sexually satisfied will be the day I die."

"You're terrible." Sherry said.

"And you love it!" Mark responded.

She did and she loved that he was back to himself again. He had a project, something to occupy his time, something to get his mind off how he was treated by the deputy a week or so ago.

Chapter 14

Over the next few days Mark got outside and worked in the yard and went out on the lake to challenge the pike living in the depths of the 60-foot-deep spring-fed lake, but he always had his notebook and pencil with him. He would be checking old notes and writing new ones with the pad balanced on his knees a pencil in one hand and the fishing rod in his other. If one of the three and a half foot pike were to take his bait he would probably drop the pencil and notebook and the fish would pull the rod out of his hands.

He was leaning towards developing a novel based on the unsolved murder of the two kids from Missouri. He thought he could use the basic premise and turn it into a love triangle gone bad and maybe have one or all of the kids involved in growing marijuana in the woods or cooking meth and selling it on college campuses. When he got to shore he would do some more research and see if anything new on the murder of the kids was on line. Although, if he was going to write a novel he probably had all the research he needed and now he just had to make stuff up, but he loved doing the research.

Sherry had him grilling brats, so he stood out on the deck and re-read his notes, alternately holding a pencil, tongs or beer bottle. He scribbled notes about the book and jotted a note to consider writing the book of a serial killer loose in the Lake of the Ozarks, terrorizing the families living along the shore. The killer could get to his victims by foot through the woods, along the back roads or by boat. "Hmmm, it has potential. I'll have to roll it over in my brain some more."

With a glass of wine and a full stomach Sherry and the dog sat down on the recliner and Mark at the computer. "I'm thinking of making the book a novel about a serial killer preying on the Midwest," Mark said to Sherry.

"Oh Mark haven't you had enough of serial killers and death? How about a nice boy meets girl, they fall in love, get married and live happily ever after kind of book?"

"Yeah," Mark said, "and then boy finds a new girl and strangles old girl for the life insurance money and dismembers her body."

Sherry just looked at her husband and shook her head. "You're nuts."

"No, I may use the Missouri killings as a spring board for a novel about some maniac wreaking havoc on the Lake of the Ozarks," Mark said opening the computer and doing a search for Lake of the Ozarks.

There was the usual chamber of commerce site with glossy photographs of people having fun at summer festivals, boats on the lake and kids on the beach. There were even some glossy photographs of large offshore powerboats racing along the lake. What Mark found most interesting was a map showing the entire lake.

He leaned back to look at the map and his mind was running possibilities of murders in the hundreds of coves, or bodies floating up from under the covered boat docks. His mind drifted to the two kids sitting in a car in the local lover's lane, locked in an embrace, saying goodbye because he had to go back to college, and making up for the time they would be apart until he got home again when the passenger side window suddenly burst into a thousand shards as bullets rained in.

"I'll be damned," Mark said slowly, "I'll be damned, I think I found another one!"

Sherry looked him, "Another what?"

"Another copycat murder."

Mark remembered from reading the *Rampage* book that David Berkowitz, the Son of Sam killer who terrorized New York City in 1976- 1977 by shooting and killing people, some of them lovers in parked cars, was just like what happened with the kids in Missouri.

Mark opened the book, found the chapter and began reading, "Son of a bitch," he said again, quietly this time. Then he re-read the entry on the Missouri State police website. "Son of a bitch!" he repeated

"Look at this Sherry," Mark said pointing to the computer screen. These kids were killed in the same manner that the Son of Sam killer killed people in 1976!"

"Where?" Sherry asked.

"Where what?"

"Where did the Son of Sam kill people?"

"Oh, he murdered people in New York, mostly in Queens and the Bronx. I wonder how Debbie Daugherty wore her hair. I bet it was long and dark," Mark said.

Sherry looked at her husband and asked, "Why, now suddenly you have a thing for long haired brunettes?"

Mark smiled and said, "No, Berkowitz focused on girls with long brunette hair. As the police figured it out and warned the public, beauty salons ran out of blonde hair dye and short wigs. I wonder if Debbie had long, dark, hair?"

Mark, with a renewed zest for murder, scribbled questions in his notebook under the heading of Missouri Murders and a subheading of Debbie Daugherty; hair color, hair length, any other ambush type shooting in the area? He printed a hard copy of the Missouri unsolved murder listing for his records. He loved computers but still liked to have a hard copy to hold in his hands.

Mark drew the horizontal and vertical lines of another "chart of death" as he came to call them. Along the top he wrote; Son of Sam and in the other column he wrote Ozarks. Below that he drew several horizontal lines, one each for all of the similarities between the two crimes; Lovers Lane, male, female, gunshots. Mark penciled in a check in both columns following each listing.

"There may not be any connection between the Ozark murders and the Son of Sam murders but I need to follow it up," Mark said to himself. "And I'm not going to be in a hurry to call the police like I was with the girl in the Green River. I don't need another cop thinking I'm some old bothersome nutcase."

That night Mark lay next to a sleeping Sherry, his mind mentally comparing likenesses of the two cases. The similarities were remarkable but he had too many unanswered questions; about the physical description of the girl in Missouri, and especially the gun. Berkowitz used a .44 caliber Bulldog revolver. "I need to find out if the weapon used in the Missouri killings was a Bulldog; I should call the police," Mark thought. "If the gun used was a Bulldog then it's almost a fact that someone is copying famous, or infamous serial killers. I've got to find the answers to these questions," Mark thought before he drifted off to sleep.

Chapter 15

"How long have you been up?" Sherry asked as she shuffled to the bathroom and Mark stood at the front door waiting for the dog.

"My usual time. I've been searching for more information about the Missouri shootings."

Sherry sat down in her recliner, the dog jumped into her lap and she reached for her morning mug of French vanilla creamer with coffee Mark had made and placed next to her chair. "Thanks," she said, holding the mug towards Mark. "I thought you were going to write a novel, Mark. It sounds to me you are spending a lot of time on the murder of the two kids, an actual non-fictional case when a novel is just a bunch of made up stuff."

Mark looked up from the laptop towards his wife and said, "I think I'm still going to write a novel but sometimes novels are based on real life. Like the similarities between the Michigan girl found floating in the Green River and the Missouri murder. I find that fascinating and I'm thinking of writing a book based on them."

After Mark did research all morning, Sherry said, "Okay, Hemingway, time to close the computer and get something done around here. We need to go to town, its shopping day!"

"Yeah, I need to get away from this for a while, nothing but dead ends today." Mark saved his work and shut the computer down, grabbed his notebook, a pencil and the iPad.

"What do you need those for? I thought you said you wanted to get away from it for a while?"

"I do, just not completely away from it."
"You're obsessed."
"Yeah, I probably am."

~ ~ ~

Groceries put away, dinner cooked and eaten and the evening wine poured, Mark and Sherry cuddled next to one another on the couch, the lights off, the flames from the fireplace providing a yellow hued reflection on the walls as the moon lit the ripples on the lake with dancing diamonds. They sat in silence, Sherry thinking about the phone call they received from their daughter announcing they were going to be grandparents. Mark sat wondering how much damage a .44 caliber round fired at close range would do to a person's head.

Chapter 16

Mark was aware of two recent murders that closely resembled murders that had occurred in the past. He suspected that someone was copying famous serial killers from the past and the information was weighing heavily on him. He felt like he was an accomplice to the crimes by not reporting them. It was the same feeling he had before he called the Antrim County Sheriff's Department to report his theory about the girl found in the Green River. However, he remembered how stupid and insignificant the detective made him feel. But the feeling of withholding evidence in two murder cases was gnawing at him and he decided he had to report his findings to someone no matter if they thought he was a conspiracy nut or the second coming of Sherlock Holmes.

The two murders he uncovered occurred in two different states; Michigan and Missouri. Mark thought of calling the state police in each state but they would only be interested in the crime that occurred in their state and probably would not care about the connection with the crimes from other states. Mark did a search for an FBI tip line and found a site called FBI Tips and Public Leads, he clicked on the site. Rather than finding a phone number to call and present his case it was a computerized site where he could write out all of the pertinent details of his theory. "This will work better," Mark thought. "I could always write out my thoughts better than expressing them verbally."

Mark began to fill out the form; first name, middle name, last name, phone number. "They better not ask for my social security number," Mark thought. "But then they probably already have it and know everything about me; it's their job to know everything."

When he was done with the basic information he came to a box where he had to write the information about the case. There was a 3000-character limit. "3000 character limit, not words but characters. Shit, it's like I'm back in the newsroom with old Ken Duff, the editor I first started working for at the Free Press. He counted each word and would make us re-write and re-write until we had it just like he wanted it within the amount of words he wanted. All of us rookie reporters hated Ken but I have to admit I learned more from Ken than I learned in any journalism class at Michigan State. We learned how to write succinctly to get the information across without wasting words.

Mark grabbed his notebook and pencil off the coffee table and thought to himself, "Okay, my theory in 3000 characters or less."

After three attempts on paper, he settled on the version he hoped would fall within the limitations and yet sufficiently present his theory. He turned to the computer and entered the paragraph into the text box. A little window at the bottom counted down the characters as he typed. When he was done he was over by sixteen characters and had to go through it and edit it some to get to the character limit.

Mark pushed the submit button and leaned back on the couch and took a sip of his coffee. "There, now I have to wait for some rookie agent to call and ask for more details. But at least I did my duty and reported suspicious criminal activity.

Chapter 17

With the coffee made and bladder emptied, Mark decided to change his morning routine. Rather than plop down on the couch and sit staring at the laptop for the next few hours, reading the newspapers and researching murders, he sat in a recliner where he could see the fireplace and when the sun rose he could look out over the lake.

Mark just stared at the flames and sipped his coffee, thinking. He was having second thoughts about writing a book. He had seen so many reporters slave over a typewriter or keyboard writing the next great American novel only to find their efforts shunned by the publishing houses. What made him think he could do it? He always considered himself a hack writer, better at research than writing. "Besides", he told himself, "just because a reporter can write a news story doesn't mean they can write a fictional story. The skillset required for one is not necessarily transferable to the other.

The sun was just breaking over the horizon in the east and the lake was like a mirror reflecting the trees on the far side. Small rings on the surface formed where insects landed and became breakfast for a hungry fish. "The circle of life," Mark said aloud. "A life must end to prolong the life of another. It's true in the animal kingdom, animals kill to eat, kill to protect themselves or their young, but not mankind. Man can kill for no reason other than the pleasure of causing pain and death."

Mark saw the Serial Killer book on the coffee table and picked it up and thumbed through the pages. "Now these sick bastards killed simply for the pleasure they derived from exerting their needs and desires on others. They didn't need to kill to eat, although some of them did practice cannibalism. They weren't protecting themselves or their young; they simply enjoyed killing, exerting their will over others in the ultimate way, taking the life of another human being."

Absentmindedly thumbing from the back forward, Mark saw the photograph of David Berkowitz and he thought about the two kids in Missouri who were doing no wrong, just enjoying one another's company, just young lovers when someone fired through the passenger side window snuffing out their lives.

The photograph of Rodney Alcala caught his attention. Alcala was suspected of murdering between 8 and as many as 130 girls and women. Ironically, he was a contestant on the television game show, The Dating Game.

Mark slowed to look at the illustrations in the chapters on Ted Bundy and Herb Baumeister. Baumeister was a successful Indianapolis businessman who murdered men he picked up in gay bars. Then as Mark continued leafing through the pages of the serial killer book, he stopped at the chapter titled; A Serial Killer Anomaly, a female serial killer. He stared at the photograph of the pretty young woman, the woman who was a nurse and murdered patients in her care by injecting their IV bags with the untraceable heart stimulant epinephrine. "Shit!" this is just like the nurse I read about a few days ago. Where did I read it?" Mark was thinking. "I wonder if this could be another copycat killing?"

He moved to the couch and opened the laptop. While the computer woke up, he flipped pages in his notebook until he found the notes he scribbled about the nurse.

"USA Today. Nurse - Veterans hospital - South Carolina arrested for suspicion of murdering several patients in her care - injecting epinephrine into their IV bags. Nurse shocked at the accusations and proclaimed her innocence."

"I've got to start another grid," Mark said. "It's another case that is following a murder written up in the serial killer book," Mark repeated slowly. "Shit, maybe the killings and the book are related; maybe the murderer is following the murders in the book. Maybe it's not just a coincidence that the crimes happening today also happened in the past and were recorded in the book."

"I know of three crimes; the girl in the Green River, the young couple in the Ozarks and now the nurse in South Carolina, all similar to chapters in the Kadar book *Rampage* as the Green River Killer in Washington State, the David Berkowitz Son of Sam murders in New York City and now the nurse. If they are not connected somehow then it is one hell of a coincidence."

Mark spent the rest of the day alternately reading chapters in the *Rampage* book and searching the Internet for any crimes that might resemble a murder written up in the book.

"Come on out and enjoy the day!" Sherry told Mark. "It's beautiful, one of the nicest days we've had this summer. Heck even the princess is laying in the sun on the deck."

"Ah, maybe in a bit, I've got something I am following up on," Mark answered. "I know what you're thinking, I'm obsessed, and you're probably right."

~ ~ ~

Sherry enjoyed the day outside as Mark sat inside, concentrated on the computer. "Mark!" Sherry practically yelled at her husband to get his attention. "You have been glued to the computer all day and that's enough. You have ignored me long enough, now go get showered, you're going to take me out to dinner!"

"Okay, I need a break from this anyway," Mark said shutting down the computer, and closing his notebook. He grabbed the glass on the coffee table and drank down the last of his drink.

"How many of those have you had today?" Sherry asked.

"I don't know, a couple I guess," Mark said as he picked the three sheets of paper off the table. Each sheet had a different grid pattern showing the similarities between the three murders he found and the three from the *Rampage* book. He looked them over quickly and stacked them neatly inside his notebook.

Sherry was walking up the stairs, her hair wrapped in a towel. Mark realized he was so engrossed he didn't notice she had come in from gardening all day and took a shower. Sherry yelled from the loft, "I certainly hope you have been working on your novel that is going to make us a bunch of money and pay for our grandchild's college education. You know we need to think about things like that now."

~ ~ ~

Dinner at the bar was great as usual but the good weather kept a lot of people at home. Bear, the bartender, said it's good weather and bad that keeps customers away. When it's bad; cold, rain or blowing snow people stay home preferring to be warm in their house or cabins and when the weather is great like today they stay home and grill dinner; fish they caught that day or burgers and dogs.

Sherry watched the bartender walk away from their table and said, "It's no wonder they call him Bear. The man is huge. What do you think, six foot five or six? He must have ripped his mother apart at birth." Pregnancy was on her mind.

Mark smiled, as he ironically took a drink of his Escanaba Black Bear beer. "This stuff is very good," Mark said looking at the bottle, "Upper Hand Brewing Company, Escanaba, Michigan. We have to look for some of this next time we go shopping."

"So what is it that has consumed you so much the last couple days?" Sherry asked, knowing that Mark was dying to tell her about it.

"Remember the girl found floating in the Green River?" Mark began and he continued to tell Sherry about the similarities of the three murder cases he had discovered and the murders in the Serial Killer Book. When Bear had cleared their dinner plates and Sherry sipped on her third glass of wine and Mark his third Escanaba Black Bear, Mark told her of his theory that not only are the murders similar to those in the book but they are following the murders in the book. "I don't think it's a coincidence that the current deaths resemble chapters in the book rather the murderer is using to guide his murders."

Sherry listened intently to her husband thinking she was happy he wasn't depressed anymore and that the nightmares had not returned in a few weeks but now the pendulum had swung in the other direction. He was so consumed with these murders and his theory that they are connected and related to a book that he can't do or think of anything else.

When Mark paused to finish his beer Sherry said, "You haven't said much about our daughter being pregnant. Mark, we're going to be grandparents. Aren't you happy about it?"

Mark could see the disappointment in his wife's face. She was right he hadn't shared in Sherry's excitement over Mickie being pregnant; he had been too wrapped up in death to enjoy birth.

Chapter 18

The next morning Mark climbed out of bed at 5:17 and wondered, "Why 5:17?" as he walked down the stairs from the loft. I used to hate Mondays when I was working but since retirement it's just another day. "Every day is a Saturday", like his friend Tom used to say when he retired. Mark opened the computer and the time, day and date illuminated. "Shoot, it's not Monday, it's Sunday."

As the coffee brewed, Mark composed an email to Mickie. He was always better at communicating in writing and he was long overdue in writing to his daughter.

> *Good Morning Princess,*
> *My baby girl is going to have a baby!*
> *Where have the years gone, where is my little pig tailed boat buddy who wanted to go on the boat every time I was going out? Where is my little girl who was never without a book in hand, my girl who was absolutely beautiful as a homecoming queen candidate, my little girl who graduated at the top of her class?*
> *Have I told you enough how proud I am of you? Have I told you enough how much I love you?*
> *And now my little girl is going to be a mother.*
> *My little girl is going to be a fantastic mother. Mom is going to be a great grandmother and I promise I will try to be the best grandfather I can be.*
> *I love you Princess!*
> *Dad*

"I know it's early but Mickie will get it when she checks her email. She always checks email and Facebook before she goes to church," he thought.

~ ~ ~

"Come on, Marky, we're going to church," Sherry yelled down from the loft, the dog sticking out from between the railing. "We really need to be better at going to church."

Mark looked up at his wife and the dog and asked, "What brought this on?"

"It's part of my decision to be better grandparents," Sherry said as she prepared to descend the stairs and shower.

Mark asked, "And what else do we need to change around here now that we are going to be grandparents?" He was afraid of what the answer might be.

"Well," Sherry said thoughtfully, "We are going to take better care of ourselves and get in better shape. I for one would like to be around when our grandchild graduates from high school and we, especially you, are going to slow down on the drinking."

"Aww, Granny, you are taking all the fun out of life. I suppose the next thing you are going to tell me is no more sex?"

"No, sex is okay, currently it's the only form of cardio workout we get. But we're going to start walking everyday too."

"Why don't we walk upstairs and give our hearts a good workout right now?"

Sherry smiled and said, "Let the dog out, I've got to take a shower."

The little dog ran to the door as Mark said, "Okay, I'll see you in the shower!"

"Mark, not now, we don't have time," Sherry protested. If we hurry we might be able to go out for breakfast before the 10:30 service. But it will be a healthy breakfast, no bacon or sausage and only that phony egg stuff."

Mark walked back to the computer mumbling, "Oh great she's on another health kick."

~ ~ ~

Sitting in the third pew from the back Mark leaned over to Sherry before the service started and whispered, "I think we are doing well on this new health kick of yours."

"Shush," Sherry quietly said.

"Let's see," Mark whispered, "I ate a healthy breakfast, but I still think a breakfast is not breakfast without bacon, and we got our cardio workout this morning in the shower."

"Shut up!" Sherry said a little louder.

Mark pulled a pencil from the rack that held the hymnals and offering envelopes and scratched some notes on his bulletin. Then when Pastor Mitch took the pulpit Mark paid attention because he had read the sermon's title. It was a subject close to Mark's heart; "Thou Shall Not Kill."

Mark made his living from murder, he spent the greater part of his life chasing killers, in retirement he spent most of his waking hours thinking about or reading about killers. Mark thought, "This sermon is speaking to me. I'm an expert on killing."

Pastor Mitch placed his hands on either side of the pulpit, surveyed the congregation of the First Methodist Church and with the dramatic air of a television evangelist, something Mark thought was lost on the small Upper Peninsula church said; "On Mount Sinai God gave the Israelites two stone tablets inscribed with instructions that we should worship only God, that we should honor our parents and keep the Sabbath holy." The pastor paused. "God also warned the Israelites of prohibitions about idolatry, blasphemy, murder, adultery, theft, dishonesty and coveting."

"We have over the past month and a half taken each of God's commandments given to man on Mount Sinai in order. The first commandment; Thou shall not have any other Gods before me! The second; Thou shall not make any graven images. Three; Thou shall not take the name of the Lord in vain. Four; Remember the Sabbath and keep it holy. Five; Honor thy father and thy mother. And today we shall discuss the Lord's sixth commandment; Thou shall not kill."

Mark scribbled a few notes on the bulletin; "Incorporate the sixth commandment in book, Thou shall not kill." Mark's thoughts drifted from Pastor Mitch to the murders he was following. He wondered, "Had the murderers had any religious upbringing. Had they learned the Ten Commandments? Did they know that the Lord took displeasure in man killing man?" Mark had tuned out Pastor Mitch until he heard him say,

"It is recorded in the bible that our Lord instructed man not to kill. It is written in Deuteronomy 5:17, Thou Shall Not Kill!"

"Deuteronomy 5:17!" Mark said aloud. "Deuteronomy 5:17, thou shall not kill!" he repeated.

Sherry looked at her husband with evil eyes saying, "Shush."

"Did you hear that?" Mark whispered. "Thou shall not kill is Deuteronomy 5:17. Thou shall not kill is 5:17!"

"Shush!" Sherry sternly said.

Mark sat in silence, not paying any attention to the pastor's sermon; instead he concentrated on the connection of his life to the Bible. He lived a life of death, killing and murder, not that he actually killed people but he was obsessed with it and the Commandment, Thou Shall Not Kill is in Deuteronomy, the fifth chapter, verse seventeen;

5:17. The exact time he woke up each morning. "Son of a bitch," Mark silently said. "It should read Thou Shall Not Sleep."

Chapter 19

The roof lights of the sheriff's and state police cars flashed and an ambulance with its lights switched off sat at the Church of the New Beginning, off Pioneer road, in rural Blackfoot, Idaho.

Sergeant Menendez pressed the release lever and the steering wheel jumped up and he slowly removed his bulk from the Idaho State Police cruiser. He scanned the crowd of people gathered; some in their church clothes, others in farm clothes. At first glance no one looked out of place. A couple of deputies were taking statements from them. Yellow "Crime Scene: Do Not Cross" tape was strung from the back of the church to the parsonage located behind. He took in the scene and made mental notes; parsonage about 75 feet behind church, no neighbors in sight, just farm fields, a freight train slowly gained speed as it rambled by on tracks about 100 yards behind the house, gravel driveway, no discernable recent tire tracks other than emergency vehicles.

He turned to a deputy and said, "Okay, fill me in."

Deputy Billy Namath pulled a small notebook from his chest pocket, flipped a few pages and said, "Ah, about twelve people arrived for the Sunday service that starts at 8:30. They were sitting in the pews waiting for the pastor to start. Pastor Mathew Reilly and his wife," the deputy checks his notes, "Diane. But they never showed up. The congregation waited fifteen minutes or so then the man over there in the gray suit," the Deputy pointed towards a man in his seventies, obviously emotionally distraught, "Hmmm, Jacob Main, walked to the parsonage to check on them. He found the pastor and his wife dead in the bedroom."

Menendez scratched his belly through his tightly stretched shirt and asked, "Anything missing?"

"Yeah, their car is gone. A 2006 blue Ford Fusion. I already requested an APB on it. Nothing yet, but there are a lot of miles of back roads."

When the medical examiner walked out of the house, Sergeant Menendez yelled, "Hey Larry!" and waved for the man to join him. The M.E., clad in a white Tyvek suit from the bottom of his shoes to the top of his head made a rustling sound as he walked. Latex gloves peeled off, the two men shook hands.

"Manny, you got a nasty one on your hands. Whoever killed the pastor and his wife was one mean son of a bitch," the M.E. said. "Both of them were beaten to death by several blows from a sledge hammer. The hammer, covered in blood, was lying next to the bed. Looks like the preacher's wife was raped too, but I won't know for sure till I get her back to the lab. The killer screwed them up pretty bad, their chests were caved in, arms broken and their faces beaten so badly they are unrecognizable. From the amount of blood it looks like the preacher died right away but his wife may have laid there for a while until she bled out."

"Thanks Larry. Make me your first call when you find something. Can I go in?"

"Better wait, I don't know if the tech boys are done yet."

Chapter 20

Monday morning Mark awoke and looked at the digital clock, it read 5:17 and the words of Pastor Mitch came back to him, "Deuteronomy 5:17; Thou Shall Not Kill."

"A coincidence? Or a message from above about my profession and obsession," Mark pondered as he climbed out of bed to begin his morning routine.

He read a couple of articles and had poured a second cup of coffee before he spotted a headline that caught his attention; Pastor and Wife Killed in Idaho. Mark read the article with his normal interest in any murder, but this one was bizarre. Mark thought, "The killer used a sledgehammer to kill his victims, striking them numerous times."

Mark got up to act out the scene. He stood over the couch as if he was the killer and the couch was the bed where the minister and his wife lay. "Let's see, the article said they were struck multiple times in the body and head, let's say three or four times in the body and the same in the head, that's 12 to 16 swings. Mark pretended to be holding a long handle sledgehammer and swung down towards the couch three times, then another three where he thought the pastor's wife might be laying.

"What in the world are you doing?" Sherry yelled from the loft railing.

Mark was brought back to reality and looked up at his wife, "Oh, good morning. Ah, I'm just working on a murder case. Sort of." Mark was so intent to kill the victims on the bed with his sledgehammer he didn't hear the dog come down or his wife get out of bed. He looked and found the dog sitting by the lakeside door with a disgusted look on its face. Sort of the same look Sherry had when she walked down. Mark pretended to put his sledgehammer down and let the dog out.

Once the fuzz face had watered the yard and jumped up in Sherry's lap she asked, "Now tell me what you were doing when I saw you beating up the couch."

Mark explained but had to admit it even sounded weird to him.

"Mark, I think you are getting stranger and stranger in your old age."

"Yeah, probably," was all Mark could reply.

Sherry looked at her husband staring at the computer screen and asked, "How could you act out killing two people on a bed when you were swinging your axe at a couch. Why don't you go to the loft and chop up your victims on our bed?"

Mark looked up at his bride and said, "You're right, it would be more realistic. And it's a sledgehammer, not an axe." Mark playfully pretended to pick up his sledgehammer and lift the heavy hammer to his shoulder and went to the loft where he could swing at his victims.

"Mark, please try not to get any blood on the sheets, I just washed them yesterday," Sherry said barely able to keep from giggling.

Sherry was right; it was much more realistic swinging an imaginary sledgehammer at a real bed. He discovered the killer had to have swung from one side then moved to the other side of the bed to pound the other person. Mark descended the stairs and thanked Sherry for her suggestion. It made a difference in understanding some of the finer details of the murders.

Sherry started singing the Beatles song, *"Bang! Bang! Maxwell's silver hammer came down upon her head. Bang! Bang! Maxwell's silver hammer made sure that she was dead."*

"Very funny," Mark said smiling at his wife. "Now that will be stuck in my head all day. Thanks a lot."

Chapter 21

The days became cooler and a couple of the nights brought frost. Mark agreed with Sherry that life in Northern Michigan was beautiful in the spring, summer and fall but he was not so fond of winter. Their first winter was brutal. Mark quickly learned that the snow blower he used to clean his drive downstate was no match for the accumulation they received in the Upper Peninsula. Mark finally hired the kid down the road to plow out their drive.

Mark was beginning to think all of his friends who went south for the winter might just have a good idea. Maybe he could talk Sherry into leaving after Christmas and staying for a month. Mark thought to himself, "I really don't think it will take much to convince Sherry."

In the last few weeks since Mickie announced she was pregnant, Sherry had gone downstate to visit her, leaving Mark to care for the dog. Mickie's husband didn't like dogs and Mark wasn't too fond of Mickie's husband. He treated Mickie well and earned a good living so Mark over looked his arrogant attitude.

Mark continued to search out murders and take notes, three notebooks so far. Writing a book was still a possibility. He spent days thinking of possible characters, scenarios, and twists and turns a plot could take.

One September evening Mark was sipping a Manhattan and thinking about his FBI tip line submission. "You would think someone would have gotten back to me, at least an email thanking me for the submission. But no, nothing." Mark wasn't going to let it bother him like before. He did what he thought he should do by alerting the FBI to a possible serial killer on the loose copying other serial killers. If they didn't want to follow it up that was up to them. "I did my duty of reporting it."

When his mother and sister came to visit, Mark had put the *Rampage* book back on the shelf. After pouring a glass of wine for Sherry, he walked to the shelf and pulled the book out and sat back on the couch. He was not so much reading it as he was looking at how it was written. He was looking for ideas on how to write his book. He was studying the mechanics of the book; dedication page, numbered chapters, or named chapters or both numbers and names, introduction, index, table of contents. "There is a lot more to a book than writing text," Mark thought, randomly turning pages. He stopped at a chapter called, "Evil contained in human form". "Now that is a catchy chapter title," Mark said thumbing through the pages and skimming the text. "No shit!" Mark almost yelled, when he came across a newspaper headline in a highlight box, "Minister, wife found slain in church parsonage."

"Sherry looked from the Sudoku book and asked, "Now what? Did you find Jimmy Hoffa?"

"No," Mark mumbled as he went to the shelf and withdrew his three notebooks labeled Murder 1, Murder 2 and Murder 3. "How could I have missed this?" Mark scolded himself.

After scanning his notes and flipping through the pages of Murder 2, he picked up Murder 3. "Here it is," Mark said aloud and began reading.

Sherry looked at her husband and just shook her head. Even the dog gave Mark a look of disgust.

Mark read a couple of weeks ago during his morning routine about a pastor and his wife who were murdered. It looked like a random murder but not many details of the crime were provided. He read his notes; Blackfoot, Idaho - Church of the New Beginning – pastor and wife murdered.

Found in parsonage behind church and the date and where he had found the information. Not much. No follow up information, no more articles that Mark found. He remembered pretending to swing a sledgehammer at the bodies on a bed; Sherry suggested he act it out up in the loft on the bed.

Mark picked up the *Rampage* book and found the chapter on Ángel Leoncio Reyes Resendez-Ramirez. In 1999 Ramirez killed a pastor and his wife in a rural Texas town. The parsonage was located behind the church and no one knew about the deaths until they didn't show up for Sunday Services. "Just like the pastor and his wife in Idaho," Mark said to himself.

Ramirez was known as the "Railroad Killer" because he jumped on freight trains for transportation. When he murdered the preacher and his wife, Ramirez had jumped from a train that ran behind the parsonage. "Are there railroad tracks behind the parsonage in Blackfoot, Idaho?" Mark checked in his notebook.

Ramirez beat the couple with a sledgehammer while they lay in bed. He also raped the wife. "I wonder if the woman in Idaho was raped? The article didn't say anything about a rape. It's time for another grid pattern to compare similarities."

"Sherry, you know these murders that are like the murders in the Serial Killer book seem to be more than just a coincidence. There are too many similarities, too many points that line up. I wonder if the author of the book has noticed the pattern."

Sherry looked at her husband and said, "Call the author and ask."

Mark looked up from the computer screen at his wife, smiled and thought, "Now why didn't I think of that?"

He picked up the book and flipped it over to the back cover. There was a photograph of the author and he read the author's biographical information. "I have his name and where he lives. I should be able to find a phone number."

~ ~ ~

A quick Internet search turned up a home address and a phone number for a person named Wayne Kadar who lived in Harbor Beach, Michigan. Mark wrote the information down in his notebook and began thinking of what he would discuss with the author of the *Rampage* book.

"What are you working on now?" Sherry asked.

"I'm taking your advice and I'm going to call the author of the serial killer book and tell him the similarities I've discovered between the killers in his book and the murders I have found."

Sherry cocked her head to the side giving her husband a smirk and said, "Oh, you're taking my advice, huh? So maybe your wife isn't so dumb. Maybe there are a few good ideas rattling around in this blonde head, huh?"

"No, you've got some good ideas, like pretending to use the sledgehammer upstairs on a real bed and calling the author were both good ideas. Keep them coming."

Mark went back to thinking of questions he might ask the author and Sherry scratched the dog behind the ears and said, "See, mommy comes up with some good ideas once in a while."

Chapter 22

The phone was answered on the fourth ring, a woman slightly out of breath from running inside. "Hello?"

"Hello, I'm calling for Mr. Kadar."

"Just a minute, he's out in the garage." Mark could hear the woman yelling, "Skip! Skip telephone. The woman came back on the line and said, "He will be here in just a minute."

"Hello, this is Skip."

Skip? Mark wondered if he had called the wrong Kadar. The book jacket said Wayne Louis Kadar. "Hello, are you Wayne Kadar, the author of *Rampage*?" Mark asked.

"Yes I am. But I go by my nickname, Skip. How can I help you?"

"I'm Mark Daniels. I'm a retired crime reporter for the Detroit Free Press and I was wondering if I can ask you a few questions about your book, *Rampage*"?"

"Sure, fire away," the author answered.

Mark began from the beginning with the discovery of the body of Bonnie Winslow found floating in a Michigan river. "The girl in the Michigan River was found nude, and her panties were stuffed in her mouth," Mark added.

"Sounds like Gary Ridgway," Kadar said.

"Exactly!" Mark said excitedly. "Like Ridgway's Green River murders. Mark saved the clincher for last. "And like Gary Ridgway's victims found in the Green River in Washington State, Bonnie Winslow was found in a river in Michigan named the Green River."

There was silence on the other end of the line. Mark asked, "Are you still there?"

"Yes, I'm just letting this absorb in."

Mark said, "Well, wait I have more."

"Hold on. I have to get something to write with. Just a minute."

While waiting, Mark got out the grid patterns he developed outlining the similarities.

"Okay, I'm ready. I want to take some notes."

Mark told him about the kids who were shot to death in Missouri's Lake of the Ozarks area and compared it to the Son of Sam murders.

Kadar asked a few questions and seemed amazed at the similarities. Next Mark told the author about the pastor and his wife in Idaho and how it corresponded to the murders of a minister and his wife in the Ramirez chapter of his book.

"Now I don't know if the murderer is copying famous murderers or copying chapters from your book, but the similarities are truly amazing," Mark said into the phone.

"Have you identified any killings that are not in my *Rampage* book or my earlier book *Great Lakes Serial Killers*? It might be just a coincidence that some nut is copying killers from the past that I chose to write about in my books. If you find a copycat murder of one I didn't write about then it would prove that he is not following my books."

Mark replied, "I fully intend to keep searching for any other murders that resemble murders from the past and if I find any more I'll let you know."

Kadar said, "Give me your name again and your phone number. I want to digest this and I'll get back to you."

Mark gave the author his information then added, "By the way, I called the police in Michigan with what I discovered about the Bonnie Winslow murder, and they politely thanked me for the information and I never heard back from them. Then I reported the similarities of the Michigan and Lake of the Ozark murders to the FBI through their tip line a few weeks ago but I have yet to hear back from them either."

The author responded, "Well, I will get back to you, I promise."

~ ~ ~

"What was all that about?" Karen, the author's wife, asked as she set a glass of iced tea next to him.

"Ah, this guy seems to think some crazy person is copying murders that I wrote about in the *Rampage* book. It's very interesting. Someone is murdering people in the same manner as serial killers of the past; very intriguing."

Kadar's wife sipped her tea thinking about what her husband had just said. "Maybe the guy who called is the crazy person, maybe he is the guy doing the murders."

Kadar looked up from his notes, "Good point. I can always count on you to have a different take on a situation."

Kadar thought as he reviewed the notes, "What if she is right and the guy on the phone is the killer. Maybe now I'm his next victim."

~ ~ ~

"Who were you talking to?" Sherry asked Mark.

"I took your suggestion and called the author of the *Rampage* book. He took my theory seriously; we had a good conversation."

Sherry looked up from her crossword puzzle book and said, "What if he is the person doing the murders? Maybe he is doing it to drum up business for book sales. Stanger things have happened, you know."

Mark stopped looking at the computer screen, looked at Sherry and thought about what she had said, "What if she is right and the author is the killer? Maybe now I'm his next victim."

Chapter 23

Mickie and Sherry decided it was time for the future grandparents to leave the "Boonies", as Mickie called their U.P. home, and travel south to visit her. Sherry right away agreed, saying they would, and then she informed Mark of their trip to Frankenmuth to visit their daughter.

Sherry was excited about the visit to help Mickie pick out the baby's bedroom furniture. Mark and Sherry told her they would buy the crib and other pieces for the room. Sherry and Mickie had plans to paint the room and sew curtains; it was going to be a fun "girls" visit. Mark was along to help with the heavy lifting.

Mark realized they would be somewhat close to where the *Rampage* author lived and gave him a call. No answer but he left a message on the answering machine; "Hello Skip, this is Mark Daniels. We are going to be visiting our daughter next week in the Frankenmuth area and I was wondering if maybe we could get together and talk?"

The following day Mark's cell rang, the phone's display announcing a call from the author. "Hi Mark, you caught me at a good time, my schedule for next week works out. What do you have in mind?"

Mark answered, "I'll be staying at my daughter's house in Frankenmuth. I can drive over to your house. Or we could meet somewhere."

"Oh no, don't drive all the way over here," Kadar said, still thinking about what his wife had said about possibly Mark being the serial killer. "I'll drive over that way. I have some shopping to do anyway. How about we meet in the food court in the mall in Bay City?"

"Okay, that sounds fine with me as long as you don't mind driving all the way across the Thumb." Mark was secretly glad they were going to meet in a public place after what Sherry said about the possibility of the author killing people to drum up book sales.

A date and time was set and both men said they looked forward to discussing the killings Mark had found and their similarities to murders in the *Rampage* book.

~ ~ ~

The drive down was uneventful. I-75 south was moving just above the speed limit and Mark's co-pilot instructed him to pull off at the outlet mall at West Branch. There were a couple of children's stores Sherry wanted to stop at and "just look at the baby clothes." Mark knew she would walk out with several bags of "onesies."

Mark left his daughter's house to meet Kadar the day the painting began. He didn't like to paint and both Sherry and Mickie knew it. Mickie's husband was at work at the GM plant where he was an engineer, a fact he never let you forget. Somehow it seemed to come up in most conversations. To Mark it was almost as bothersome as him making sure everyone knew he graduated from the University of Michigan.

Mark gathered up his notebooks, a couple of pencils and his grid charts of murders. He planned to get to the mall early and get an order of sweet and sour chicken and fried rice from the Asian Pagoda in the food court. He loved it and Sherry didn't and she always reminded him it wasn't good for his type 2 diabetic body.

As arranged with the author, Mark found a table near the big clock, and as he enjoyed his decadent lunch he reviewed his notes for the hundredth time. A man sitting by himself with papers and notebooks spread all over the table must have been obvious because Kadar bought a diet

Coke, looked around and walked right up to Mark's table and asked, "Mark?"

Mark jumped up and shook the man's hand and they sat down. The men were dressed pretty much the same as all the rest of the men in the mall, jeans, button down shirt, light jacket, the same as any serial killer not wanting to draw attention to themselves would dress, Mark thought. They exchanged the normal pleasantries; "It's nice to finally meet, I hope traffic wasn't bad this morning, I loved your book."

"I did some research on you and read some of your work too," the author said. "You have quite a portfolio of murders in your past."

Mark figured Kadar would check out his credentials with the Free Press. It was a smart thing to do. Mark had done a Google search on the author as well. Mark liked to think of it as being cautious not him being paranoid, but Sherry's comment about Kadar being the killer stuck in his mind.

As they sat and talked, a man walked up to their table carrying a tray of Burger King lunch fare. The author said, "Oh Mark, this is a friend of mine, Eric Holms. I invited him to join us this morning."

Mark stood to shake his hand. The man, about two inches taller than Mark, balanced the tray with one hand and took Mark's outstretched hand. Mark gathered his papers to make room and the three men sat at the small round table.

Kadar explained that Eric helped out with distribution and marketing of his books. "I thought it would be good for Eric to join us in this conversation. I filled him in a little about what's going on but why don't you start from scratch."

Mark began as he had with the author, the F.B.I. and the Antrim County deputy before that, with the girl found floating in a river in Michigan. Eric was more than an observer, Mark noticed. He was active in the conversation and asked questions. Mark proceeded to the nurse arrested and the similarity of the nurse in the book who was killing her patients. He next told the men of the comparison between the murders of the young kids in Missouri and how they compared to the Son of Sam killings in New York. Mark concluded almost an hour later with the chart of the Idaho preacher and his wife being beaten to death and the minister and his wife who were murdered in Texas by Ramirez.

The author sipped his drink and it made a slurping sound indicating all that remained was ice as he looked at Mark's notes. Eric sat staring at the chart of similarities of the Son of Sam murder and Mark sat quiet letting the men absorb the information. "I made copies of all of this for you," Mark said. "Sorry Eric, I only made one copy."

"That's okay," he said. "I'll make copies from Skip's copy."

Mark turned to Eric, "How long have you been in the publishing business?"

"I'm not in publishing. I help out Skip with his books; I'm in retailing. I work for the Dumaro Corporation. They own the Pump, Party and Play chain of gas stations and party stores."

Mark thought for a minute. "He isn't in the publishing business. I bet Kadar was afraid to be alone with me and brought the big guy along as a bodyguard. He probably thought I was the murderer and needed backup, or that I suspect he is the killer and getting close to exposing him and he brought Eric along to take me out." Mark's imagination was running wild. Mark asked, "Eric, what do you think of all this?" his arms spreading over the papers on the table.

"I don't know, I really don't know. It might be a bunch of coincidental crap but it may also have some credibility. I really have to think about it. But to be honest if this gets out into the press it will create a huge interest in *Rampage* and sell a shitload of books."

The author said, "I don't mind selling a bunch of books but I think if someone is murdering people..." Kadar stopped and looked around to make sure no one at nearby tables was listening to their conversation, then continued more quietly, "... then the lives of innocent people is more important and we need to turn our attention to the deaths of those people and catch whomever is killing them and not worry about the book sales."

Mark gathered up the papers lying on the table, stuffed them in his canvas bag and pulled out a stapled stack of papers and handed it to Kadar. "At this time I think it would be best if this information stayed between us," Mark said and the other two men agreed.

They stood, shook hands and promised to stay in touch. Mark walked towards the east entrance and Skip and Eric walked towards the south parking lot. Mark was glad they were parked in a different parking lot just in case Eric was along to kill the man who uncovered the fact that the author was actually the murderer.

Justin Maxwell

Chapter 24

On the way back up I-75 Sherry was talkative. She went on and on about what she and Mickie had done in the baby's room, about the furniture they had picked out and would be delivered in a week or so and about the baby's name. They had scoured the two baby name books Mickie had bought and told Mark the possibilities. "Mickie and Robert are leaning towards older names, you know not trendy ones that are popular now."

Mark knew this, since at dinner the night before he was asked about names of his relatives just in case there was one that Mickie and Robert might like. Mark told them of his aunts in Wisconsin he used to visit as a kid. He had great memories of them and suggested their names for consideration for his grand offspring. "Let's see, I had Aunt Tillie, Aunt Alma, Aunt Beda and Aunt Bertha. They are all great girls names." Mickie rolled her eyes at her father. "Oh and I had an Aunt Effie, and my grandmother's name was Lagarta Hildegarde."

Mickie looked at her father and said, "We are considering naming the baby an older name but not an ancient name, not a name that the poor kid will be ridiculed for having. We don't want her beat up every day at school you know. I'm sorry dad, but I'm sure Robert won't like any of those names and frankly, I am not all that enthused about them either."

"But if the baby is a boy I had an Uncle Arnold, and cousin Festus."

Sherry and Mickie just shook their heads and returned to their dinner and discussing baby names.

~ ~ ~

As Mark drove closer to the outlet mall at West Branch on the way home, Sherry asked if they could stop. "I figured you would want to stop. In fact, the car seems to pull towards the right as we get close to the exit," Mark said as he flipped on the turn signal.

While Sherry was giving the VISA a work out in the Carter's children's wear store, Mark sat in the car with the dog. The spoiled little fur ball stood up at the passenger's side window staring at the door Sherry went in and getting nose prints all over the glass. Mark pulled out his notebook. He began to scribble questions he had been thinking of on the drive while Sherry was talking about the baby and its bedroom, its bedroom furniture and its name.

"Why did Eric, Kadar's friend, attend?" Mark thought. "The guy did contribute to the conversation but most of what he said was negative. Every time Mark brought up a similarity between murders in the news and murders Kadar had written about Eric would come up with excuses of why the murders and the chapters in *Rampage* were similar. He considered almost everything a coincidence."

"I don't like him," Mark thought to himself. "I would rather just talk with Kadar. He seems more reasonable, more open to discuss the theory not just right away get all negative and not even consider the possibilities. I don't like him," Mark repeated.

Sherry walked out of the Carter's store with a bag hanging from her hand. She looked towards the car and raised a hand with her index finger up indicating she wasn't done shopping and walked towards the Gymboree store. The dog saw her and became agitated, jumping up and down, pawing at the window and barking. "Fuzz nuts, you better not pee on the seat," Mark warned the dog.

"I wonder if the author brought his friend along because he was worried about meeting with me alone.

Maybe I had insulted him by comparing his book to the murders I had uncovered. Maybe he was afraid I was some kind of writer's groupie stalking him, some kind of nut. Or maybe he invited Eric along because he wanted another set of ears to listen, another brain to analyze what I was proposing."

I wish I had someone to share this with, to discuss it with, someone who could agree or disagree, someone removed from the topic that could listen with a subjective ear. Mark thought about Pete Kazenski, the retired Detroit cop who Mark befriended. He would have been happy to listen to the theory with a subjective ear. In the past during their careers, Mark did run some thoughts by him on articles he was writing and Pete was great at taking everything in, making a few phone calls, doing some research, and being open and honest with his response. I wish I could call Pete now, but all those Camel non-filtered cigarettes he smoked one after the other took their toll and lung cancer finally beat the big guy. I need someone like Pete, a confidant, someone who wouldn't be afraid to tell me I'm full of shit."

The little Yorkie fur ball began jumping, barking and scratching at the window again alerting Mark that Sherry had exited the store. He put his notebook on the back seat and checked the passenger's seat for doggy dribble.

"You would not believe the great deals I found," Sherry said as she put three shopping bags in the back seat.

Mark and Sherry thought since Mickie and Robert had been married for almost eight years and they didn't have children they had decided not to have any, so they were happily surprised when the kids made the birth announcement.

As Mark merged with the northbound traffic of I-75, Sherry excitedly began to tell him what she had bought. Struggling to remember it all, she reached in back and grabbed a bag and began pulling little outfits out for Mark to look at. Sherry emptied the contents of all three bags holding up each outfit, and proudly telling Mark how much she saved. "Everything was on sale!"

Mark smiled at his wife and said, "Of course everything was on sale, it's an outlet mall. It's supposed to be on sale."

The fashion show continued for miles and it took Mark's mind off the meeting with the author and Eric. He enjoyed seeing Sherry so excited. Mark knew they had fallen into a very lazy way of life since they moved to the Upper Peninsula. He had his hobby of following murders but Sherry didn't have much outside of tending her flower garden, Facebook and Sudoku. Ever since Mickie and Robert announced their pregnancy Sherry had been a new person. The impending grandchild had so excited her that it was all she talked about. She said she even dreamt she was holding the baby. She told Mark all about the dream; "I was sitting in my chair next to the fireplace and the sleeping baby was wrapped in a pink blanket in my arms. "Pink! Mark, does that mean the baby is a girl? I dreamt the baby was in a pink blanket; I bet she is a girl."

They stopped in Mackinaw City for dinner at Darrow's Family Restaurant; it was their favorite place in Mackinaw City to eat. They have been known to plan their trips north or south around a stop at Darrow's making sure they left early enough or late enough so they would be at Darrow's for lunch or dinner. While waiting for their meals, Sherry checked Facebook and Mark read a brochure about the building of the Mackinaw Bridge. The bridge always fascinated him.

The Mackinaw Bridge is a 5-mile-long suspension bridge crossing the 295-foot-deep Straits of Mackinaw, and connecting Lower Michigan to the Upper Peninsula. The brochure gave a lot of pertinent facts about the bridge, like that it took seven years from the time of congressional approval to its dedication in 1957. In 1984, the bridge celebrated the 50 millionth crossing and the 100 millionth in 1998, there are 4,851,700 steel rivets, 1,016,600 bolts in the bridge and that the bridge weighed 1,024,500 tons. All important facts but Mark in his warped mind wondered how many jumpers had taken their last step from the bridge.

They finished their meals and Sherry insisted they pass on the homemade pie and rejoined the cars on I-75 and climbed the approach to the Mackinaw Bridge to cross over to the Upper Peninsula. Mark looked to the east and watched the ferry carrying its passengers to and from Mackinaw Island, one of the premier tourist attractions of the Midwest. Out the left window Mark watched a freighter heading west, probably with a load of iron ore for the steel mills at Gary, Indiana.

As they drove along US 2, the east-west highway along the top of Lake Michigan, Sherry was talking with Mickie on the phone and Mark's thoughts went back to the meeting at the Bay City Food Court. "When I first talked to Kadar and again when we met at the mall he seemed very receptive to the idea that the murders were connected to the *Rampage* book or at least they were murders that seemed to also appear in the *Rampage* book. However Kadar's friend Eric was very dismissive of the idea, leaning more towards the coincidence theory. "I really think there is some connection between the murders and the book. There are just too many parallels to discount," Mark thought to himself.

Chapter 25

Sherry woke up around her usual time, between eight and nine o'clock. She wasn't nearly as habitual as her husband. The dog jumped from the bed as Sherry swung her legs off. Sherry took a good morning stretch and the dog did the same. She pulled her robe on and stepped into her slippers as the dog bounced down the stairs to go outside. It was the only time in the day the dog was eager to see Mark.

Mark wasn't waiting by the door; he was deep in thought looking at the laptop. The dog stared at Mark. She didn't understand since he was always at the door ready to let her out. It was his job. Impatient, the dog barked once at Mark to remind him it was time for her to go out. "Okay, okay. Come on you overgrown dust bunny, I'll let you out."

"Are you writing the novel?" Sherry asked as she sat down with her French Vanilla and dog.

"I'm trying. I'm working on the first sentence of the first chapter. I want it to be something that grabs your attention and makes you want to read the rest of the book no matter how crummy it is. *Call me Ishmael*" and, *"It was the best of times and the worst of times..."* have already been used." Mark said with a smile.

Sherry said, "How about, *'Scarlett O'Hara was not beautiful, but men seldom realized it when caught by her charm...'*?"

Mark smiled at his wife and said in his best Rhett Butler voice, "Frankly Sherry, I don't give a damn."

"What did you put in my coffee? This tastes different, good but different," Sherry asked.

"I added a little Irish Cream to the mix this morning. I thought I'd shake up our day." Mark took a sip of his coffee, also spiked, and thought, "Shit now all I can think about is *Gone with the Wind* or *A Tale of Two Cities*."

Throughout his career Mark had been stumped for a good opening line many times, but in the fast paced world of a major daily newspaper it didn't allow for wasted time. Mark was sure he would figure something out. "Maybe I should just start writing and worry about the details later in the rewrite," Mark decided.

Sherry sat in her chair slowly scratching the sleeping dog's stomach and catching up on what was happening on Facebook. Mark stared out the windows towards the lake and an idea came to him. He moved the cursor and typed a few strokes and up popped several websites with maps of the Lake of the Ozarks. He was just going to start and see where it took him. "What the hell, if I hit a dead end, I'll just start over."

By lunch he had written about five pages about a man and woman who pull their Camaro into the garage of a nice home about three miles from the lake. The house wasn't some run down shack with an old snowmobile that had sat in the front yard for two years, or an old pickup rusting in the driveway. Neighbors and passersby would never know it was a meth house.

After lunch Mark was in the process of developing his characters, Dave and Pam Mackenzie; clean cut, well-dressed, not the stereotypical people you expect to find cooking meth; not long stringy unwashed hair, rotten teeth, bad complexion meth heads.

By dinner Mark was researching how to cook Methamphetamine from doing a Google search. "It's amazing what you can find on the internet if you look," Mark thought. "The ingredients, the proportions, the entire recipe on how to make the highly addictive drug is right there for anyone to see. I wonder if I can find out how to make a nuclear bomb on the internet?" he thought.

When Sherry yelled from the kitchen that dinner was ready, Mark clicked save, sending his day's worth of toil to a corner of the computer to be retrieved the next morning.

Over a pot roast that sat in a crock-pot all day, Sherry asked how the book was coming.

"I'm moving along rather well," Mark said. "Of course I'm only doing background work now. What do you want to know about making Methamphetamine? Go ahead, ask me anything. I'm an expert in cooking Meth."

Sherry chewed a bit of tender meat and said, "I don't even know what it is."

"Well, my dear, you came to the right place. I'll be glad to enlighten you about the chemical combination that is used mainly in the United States and Asia recreationally as an aphrodisiac and euphoria producing drug. Did you know methamphetamine has the ability to increase energy and increase sexual desire to the point that users are able to engage in sexual activity continuously for several days?"

"Oh God, too much of even a good thing is too much," Sherry said. "What's it used for in the first place?"

Mark smiled and said, "Well, I'm glad you asked. The FDA approved the drug in low doses for the treatment of attention deficit hyperactivity disorder and obesity in adults and children, but at higher doses it can cause psychosis, seizures and cerebral hemorrhage, unpredictable, rapid mood swings, delusions and violent behavior."

"Uck, please change the subject," Sherry asked.

That evening Mark left the computer off and cuddled on the couch with Sherry, a glass of wine and the dog. He hugged her close, his hand brushing the side of her breast and her hand rested on his thigh. She finished the wine, set the glass on the coffee table, grabbed Mark's arm and said, "Come on. Let's go upstairs." Mark quickly finished his wine and got up off the couch, took his wife in his arms for an embrace and deep kiss. Sherry looked into his eyes and said, "But don't expect this sexual activity to last continuously for several days!"

Chapter 26

Three days passed before Mark heard back from the author of *Rampage*. "Mark, I have been doing some research on the murders you told me about and how they compared to murders in the book, and I have some thoughts."

"Sure, Skip, what have you found?"

"Well, I discussed the whole copycat scenario at length with Eric, my friend you met, and we are not so sure the murders and similarities aren't just coincidences, some remarkable coincidences, but just the same coincidental at best. Take the girl found in the river in Michigan; the girl was a known prostitute and prostitutes are the victims of many serial killers. Sex plays a major role in the mind of the serial killer. Look at Jeffery Dahmer, John Wayne Gacy and Richard Speck, some of the more infamous killers in recent times. They were all driven by sex. They raped and murdered their victims and performed perverse sadistic sexual rituals with their corpses afterward."

"But what about the panties being stuffed in her mouth?" Mark asked.

"Yeah, I thought about that too," Kadar said. "The fact that the panties were stuffed in her mouth is not common yet it's not an unheard of method of demeaning what the killer considers an unclean woman, a woman in the sex trade. The killer might have deep psychological issues with females and a need to express his authority over what he considers the weaker sex."

"But the body was disposed of in a river named the Green River," Mark mentioned.

The author responded, "In the research I have done over the past several years on the two books I have written about serial killers I found that the serial killer does not necessarily operate out a lot of forethought in selecting a place to dispose of a victim. Rather, where the victim is left is often an opportunistic decision. The girl might have been left in that particular river because it was a remote, secluded location, not just because it was named the Green River."

The author changed the topic to the murder in the Lake of the Ozarks. "The kids shot to death in the Lake of the Ozarks area is again a crime which closely resembles the Son of Sam murders but I'm not sure it was done by a person intentionally making his murder look like a murder in the *Rampage* book." Kadar continued, "Eric has been there a couple of times and he told me that the area is beautiful and a Mecca for water craft enthusiasts of all kinds, but the area does have a sinister side too. He said there have been several drug busts and, like many rural areas, there seem to be a lot of meth labs cropping up in back woods cabins being a remote area where you can easily hide such illegal activity. Maybe the shooting is drug related. And I haven't heard of there being any other similar killings in the area. It's probably the work of some deranged person acting alone with a grudge against the kids that were killed."

Mark thought about what he had just heard and said, "Have you heard of any other murders that take place on a lover's lane?"

"Well, actually in the book under the chapter of Serial killers from around the world, I wrote about a man who preyed on couples in Italy. He killed seven or eight couples while they were romantically engaged in parked automobiles."

Mark said, "I came across another murder which seems to resemble one from your book. It's a nurse who was found injecting her patients with a drug that killed them, and you have a chapter about a nurse who does just that."

The author thought and said, "In fact there are two chapters in *Rampage* about nurses who kill patients in their care. It's the angel of mercy syndrome. But again, while it is not common, it is not a crime that hasn't occurred in the past."

Mark was out of rebuttal. He realized that Eric's negativity had crept into Kadar. Eric had gotten to him. He thanked the author for getting back to him and promised to call him if he found any other crimes of interest.

"I don't like Eric," Mark said to himself.

Chapter 27

Mark sat in the aluminum rowboat drifting along the lake on a gentle breeze. It was a cool early fall day but the lake was still fishable. He watched his bobber floating on the surface and thought, "I'm not going to let that get me down. Okay, maybe my theory is a bunch of hogwash. A poor choice of words for a guy who is afraid of pigs," he thought. "Maybe the theory doesn't hold water," Mark changed it to, then decided for a guy sitting in a boat in the middle of a lake it wasn't the best choice either.

"But the whole copycat serial killer sounds like a likely scenario to me but maybe I'm looking too deep into the subject to see the obvious like the cop in Antrim County, the FBI and the author of *Rampage*. Oh well, I have other fish to fry." He watched his bobber floating motionless on the water and said, "Well, I hope to have other fish to fry."

Mark wished he had brought his notebook to review the notes he had taken, not about copycat serial killers but notes he had scribbled for book possibilities. "Maybe I'll start from scratch. Throw out the notes and think about a boy meets girl novel like Sherry said. I bet I could write a pretty erotic novel. Sherry is always saying I have a dirty mind."

"Any luck?" Sherry asked as Mark came in from the boat and sat in the recliner facing the fireplace and avoiding the computer.

"Nope, the fish aren't hungry today," He said as he turned on the computer and opened the Detroit News website finding an article about disgraced ex-mayor Kilpatrick filing another appeal to get out of federal jail.

"Well I'm getting hungry," Sherry said, "Do you want to cook burgers on the grill or take me out to dinner?" Sherry already knew his choice. It was Wednesday and parmesan-encrusted whitefish was the special at the Jack Pine.

Reading the article, Mark answered, "Sure."

"Sure what? I gave you two choices," Sherry said.

Awaking from a thought Mark asked, "Ah, what were the choices, again?"

"I said," Sherry started. "Never mind, get cleaned up, we're going out for dinner."

Over dinner Mark told Sherry about his latest conversation with the author of *Rampage*. Mark was honest and admitted that maybe his theory was way off base. But he enjoyed doing the research and wasn't upset. He told her that, if nothing else, it cleared his mind to begin writing the novel.

"Great!" Sherry said. "What's it going to be about?"

Mark took a sip of his beer and said, "I'm thinking of taking your suggestion and writing a nice boy meets girl novel. It will take place up here in the U.P. where there are miles and miles of forests. I'm thinking of calling it *Thirty Seven Shades of Green*: An erotic tale of sex and depravity in the rich green woods of the Hiawatha National Forest; senior citizens camping at Tahquamenon Falls jumping from trailer to trailer in some sexual frenzy, and fishermen and fisherwomen frolicking on a deserted island in Munising Bay. I may throw in a chapter about nudists walking the Mackinaw Bridge during the annual Labor Day bridge walk, and bird watchers in search of the elusive Woodcock," Mark said with a wink.

Sherry looked at Mark, glad there weren't any diners close enough to overhear their conversation and said, "You're goofy."

Mark replied as their daughter did when she was a child, "Well, you're Mickey Mouse."

Sherry was happy that the bad news from the author hadn't resulted in Mark becoming depressed. They laughed and joked about the book and went home and relaxed in front of the fireplace sharing a bottle of red wine. They were happy; he was relaxed, like a giant weight had been lifted off his shoulders. They made love by the moonlight and fell asleep in each other's arms. Mark slept soundly until the pigs crawled out of his subconscious and haunted his slumber.

Throughout his career, Mark had covered hundreds of deaths and murders, some gruesome deaths others just the normal drug related drive by killings.

He covered for the newspaper sensational cases like in the summer of 1991 when he was sent to Milwaukee where a black man was found wandering around the streets with handcuffs locked on one hand. He told the police a wild tale about a man who was trying to kill him and offered to take the police to the guy's apartment.

A clean-cut well-spoken white man, Jeffery Dahmer, answered the door and invited in the police and the handcuffed man. The first thing they noticed about the apartment was the horrible stench of stinking garbage, but an apartment smelling of garbage was not unusual in that neighborhood.

Dahmer explained to the officers that there wasn't anything bad going on, that he and the man were just playing a sex game that involved the handcuffs. One of the cops went into Jeffery's bedroom to get the handcuff key and noticed a pile of Polaroid photographs. The photographs were of men and boys, some posing, some sleeping, some dancing nude, some that looked dead. Some photographs were of bodies in various states of dismemberment. The cop found a photograph of a severed head in a refrigerator. He walked to the kitchen, opened the refrigerator door slowly, knowing what he would find; a dead lifeless head stared back at him.

In Jeffery Dahmer's apartment, the police found, in addition to the head in the refrigerator, three more human heads wrapped in plastic bags in the freezer compartment. On a closet shelf in Dahmer's bedroom were two human skulls, and Dahmer's collection included formaldehyde filled jars preserving several male penises.

Dahmer even performed medical experiments on some of his victims by drilling holes in the heads of the drugged men and boys then poured muriatic acid into their brains, trying to create a zombie that would remain his sex slave forever.

In an act of ultimate control over his prey, Dahmer engaged in acts of cannibalism. Found in the freezer along with the heads were several freezer bags of human flesh. Dahmer said that he would cut the biceps and other muscles from the bodies of his victims and store them in freezer bags so he could eat them later. Dahmer admitted he experimented with various spices and meat tenderizers in an effort to make the meat more palatable.

As perverse, as depraved, as disgusting as the crimes of Jeffery Dahmer were, they were not the cause of Mark's nightmares.

In 1966, Mark was still in college studying journalism and he covered the murders of the sick bastard Richard Speck for the school newspaper. Speck spent a night terrorizing, raping, and killing student nurses in Chicago. As gruesome as the murders were and the fact that the girls killed were of his age was troubling to Mark but not nightmare producing.

In the late seventies and early 1980's, Mark wrote an article on the murders of Ray Norris and Lawrence Bittaker, the "Tool Box" murderers, who sadistically killed girls and young women and mutilated them with pliers and other tools from their tool box. As heinous and horrific as their crimes were, it was not Norris or Bittaker who crept into Mark's mind when he slept.

The case that did live deep within Mark's subconscious and haunted him as he slept were the murders of two Detroit area men, Brian Ognjan and David Tyll.

Ognjan and Tyll went north for a weekend during Michigan's annual migration of deer hunters in November 1985. When the men didn't return, their families became concerned and notified the police. An investigation didn't turn up any evidence of the two 27-year-old men; no firearms, no car, no bodies. They simply disappeared.

At the Free Press, Mark was given the assignment and covered the investigation from the beginning. He made several trips up I-75 to Mio, a small town in the Huron National Forest to follow the progress of the disappearance of the men. Over the years, Mark wrote numerous articles about the case and interviewed several local people but the locals weren't talking. It was as if they knew something but were afraid to speak openly about the disappearance of the men.

The Michigan State Police were the lead investigators and over the course of their investigation they used everything at their disposal to try to solve the disappearance of the men; disappearance, because the bodies of Brian Ognjan and David Tyll were never found. The area around Mio has dozens of lakes and rivers which were searched for evidence of the men; their luggage, their rifles, even the car they drove up north was missing.

The State Police brought in ground penetrating radar, excavated suspicious tracks of open fields, searched the area with aircraft and brought in cadaver dogs to search for the missing men, all without success. The case of the men who had gone north for a fun weekend of deer hunting grew cold and days turned to weeks, weeks to months, and months to years. Mark followed the case through the years and wrote update articles on the 5th, 10th and 15th anniversary of the disappearance of the men. Yet the senseless disappearance of the men always stayed with him. It crawled into the deep recesses in the back of his brain and set up camp and would creep out occasionally to remind Mark that Dave and Brian were still missing.

Eighteen years after the men disappeared there was a break in the case. A Michigan State Police detective went to interview Barbara Boudro, a woman who was at the bar the night Tyll and Ognjan went missing. She had told the police she saw the men at the bar and that they were really drunk, and that was all she knew. But the years of being silent had weighed on her and she couldn't contain what she knew any longer. She told the detective she had witnessed Ray and Don, the Duvall brothers, kill David Tyll and Brian Ognjan.

She told the police that she and a man she was with at the bar that night went back to his place. They heard a commotion outside and looked out the window where they witnessed the Duvall brothers clubbing Tyll and Ognjan with a baseball bat, beating them with their fists and kicking and stomping them when they fell to the ground. The Duvall's warned Barbara and her friend that if they told anyone about the murders they would be next. For the next eighteen years the local bullies kept their secret through fear and intimidation.

There were many rumors, some bearing hints of the truth, some more urban legend. But for eighteen years the brothers threatened to beat or kill anyone who suggested any knowledge of the crime.

The long term girlfriend of Ray Duval and mother of two of his children was said to know about the beatings of the two hunters and that the Duvall's had committed the crime, and sometimes during a heated argument she would threaten Ray that she would tell the police. She was found dead on a rural road; she had been hit by a car. No one was arrested in the hit and run accident.

The man Barbara was with that night and who also witnessed the murders died before he could testify against the brothers. He was found on a backcountry road, his head crushed, run over by a car or truck.

Once the police had Barbara as a witness, the prosecutor issued an arrest warrant for Raymond and Donald Duvall in the deaths of David Tyll and Brian Ognjan. A jury of six men and six women filled the juror's box in Arenac County Circuit Court and Mark was there to report on it for the Free Press. Mark hoped the court proceeding would bring a guilty verdict and be the last time he had to write about the two poor hunters who traveled north for a weekend of fun and hunting but never returned.

During the proceedings several witnesses opened up about the brothers and their decades of intimidation. They testified that they overheard the brothers telling how they killed the two hunters. They said the Duvall's talked about how they reduced the hunter's vehicle to parts and sold them off like they did with so many other junk cars. Witnesses also told how the brothers boasted about how they disposed of David Tyll and Brian Ognjan's bodies. The two sadistic killers bragged about taking the bodies of the hunters back to their farm and cutting the men up into small pieces and feeding the parts to their pigs.

Mark researched the concept of a pig eating a human and found that pigs will consume almost anything. He found there were records of starving pigs attacking and eating a farmer as he fed them. Mark interviewed a Michigan State University agricultural department professor and learned that a pig can and will eat human remains. They cannot digest human hair or teeth but a pig will devour human flesh and have the capability to pulverize even the large human bones with their powerful jaws. That was the night Mark suffered his first pig nightmare.

In October 2003, the Duvall brothers were found guilty of the murder of the two hunters and sentenced to life in prison without parole. The defense attorneys claimed it was a miscarriage of justice; there were no bodies, no murder weapons, his clients were convicted on hearsay and very thin circumstantial evidence. He promised an appeal. The witnesses and people of the Mio area could relax knowing that the bullies that terrorized the area were put away behind bars for the rest of their life.

The parents, relatives, wife and fiancé of the victims could gain some degree of closure. But it was Mark Daniels, the Free Press reporter who would live with the haunting memory of the hunters being brutally murdered, their bodies chopped up into small pieces and consumed by pigs.

Chapter 28

Mark put the whole serial killer theory out of his mind. It was a thing of his past and he vowed to move forward and dedicate his attention to his novel. On a shopping trip to Marquette, the largest city in the U.P., Mark went to the office supply store and bought a new notebook, his favorite, the kind with the wire spiral at the top, and a 2-pack of mechanical pencils. Mark, being a creature of habit, bought Pentel, 0.9 mm lead, Quicker Clicker, the pencil he had used for years. He knew a new notebook and pencil wouldn't help him write the book but they made him feel good, made him feel like an author. Mark would write the text on the laptop but he recorded notes in the notebook and when he and Sherry were out he took the notebook to write in when he had a thought and then would later transcribe his scribbles onto the laptop. A perfect mix of old school and new technology, he thought.

Sherry wanted to spend a few minutes "just looking" at baby clothes so Mark knew it wouldn't be just a few minutes nor would she be just looking, so he opted to sit in the car with his new notebook and pencil and write.

~ ~ ~

Before long Mark and Sherry fell back into their relaxing pattern, him researching and writing on the couch and Sherry in her chair playing on the iPad or doing Sudoku with one of Mark's new pencils she stole, as her overgrown hairy rodent lay on her lap.

He was happy with how the book was progressing. It was all still background information on the Lake of the Ozarks and character development but he was enjoying it.

He found it amazing how much information could be found on the Internet. He was thinking of having one of his characters be a pilot, although he himself had never flown a single engine aircraft. A quick Google search and Mark found a couple of sites that described in detail how to fly a small aircraft.

"So do you have the book all figured out?" Sherry asked.

"No, I have the protagonist and the first twelve pages but as of now I have no idea where it will go."

"Well, how can you write a book if you don't know what's happening, who the characters are and how it ends?" Sherry asked confused. "You can't take a trip without knowing where you're going and how you're going to get there," she said.

"I have a couple of scenarios I'm going to explore, but for the most part I'm going to start writing and just see where it goes. Sort of wing it. Something I could never do at the Free Press. There I was given an assignment, usually a maximum length, had to stay within topical guidelines and meet a deadline. Those were the limitations. On this I can take as long as I want, go off on tangents and have fun. I think I am going to enjoy this."

Sherry looked at her husband and asked, "Do you think it will sell?"

"You know, at this point I don't really care. I'm just having fun writing it. If it makes a few bucks then good, but I'm not doing it for the money, I'm doing it for me, my piece of mind, my enjoyment."

Mark was learning all he could about the Lake of the Ozarks and a thought struck him that maybe his protagonist should murder people in various locations throughout the country. Maybe he, or she, could be a travel agent and travel all around the country. "I'm going to have to think about this. It would mean I need to rework everything I have written already but I can still use some of it."

Chapter 29

"The damn internet is out again. I'm running to the country store to get a couple of newspapers. Do you need anything?" Mark yelled to Sherry as she slowly got out of bed. The dog ran down the stairs and Mark waited to let it out.

"Check to see if we have enough French Vanilla. I know we were running low," Sherry yelled from the loft. Mark mumbled to himself, "We should buy the stuff by the case."

Mark let the dog in telling it, "You better be nice to me, I'm your bodyguard. That eagle would love to eat your furry little ass." Then he yelled upstairs, "Okay, I'll be right back." The dog ran up the stairs and jumped in bed. Mark knew Sherry was awake but not ready to get up yet. He thought to himself, "I bet she stays in bed until she hears me drive back into the driveway. No big deal, we are just on different schedules. She sleeps in and I wish I could." He thought a minute and mumbled, "5:17 Thou Shall Not Sleep!" Then he added, "and don't kill anyone either."

Mark picked up a Marquette Mining Journal and a Milwaukee Journal, some French vanilla coffee creamer and a four pack of fresh baked butter rum muffins.

"I'm home!" Mark yelled, expecting Sherry to still be in bed but he heard the shower running. "The queen has risen." The dog walked to the door not to welcome him home but rather to see who had walked in. "No growling, no barking, what kind of watch dog are you?" The dog gave Mark a disinterested look and walked back to assume its sentinel position outside the bathroom door.

Mark poured a cup of coffee and made Sherry her French vanilla concoction then went to the couch. He turned on the computer, hoping the Internet had been restored, but no. Mark gave a disgusted sigh and unfolded the Milwaukee Journal.

Along the left side was a column listing headlines and a synopsis of articles contained within. "Sort of a teaser," Mark thought. Running a finger down the column he read the list; City council news, Capitol Report from Madison and others that didn't interest Mark, until he read the last entry.

Body Found in Sun Prairie
A female body was found in rural Sun Prairie
by two hunters.
Foul play is suspected. Pg. 2 Col. 1

Mark turned to page 2 and found the article in column 1 and began reading.

MADISON - The body of a University of Wisconsin – Madison coed was found in rural Sun Prairie. The girl had sustained a severe beating, she had welts from being lashed with a leather belt, the belt buckle leaving deep wounds on her body. The woman was an 18-year-old freshman at the university. The lead detective said it looked as though the girl was murdered in a different location and placed where she was found.

The rest of the article was a summary of previous bodies that had been found. The police had not made public any connection of the three dead girls found over the past four months. Two of the dead girls were students at the University of Wisconsin and one was a sophomore at Edgewood College in Madison.

"Sounds like they're connected to me," Mark thought. "Three murders in four months, all female, all coeds. Yeah, they sound connected to me. I think there is a serial killer on the loose in Madison."

Mark did more research looking for articles about the previous two murders. He got out his notebook and pencil and scribbled notes under the topic, "Dead Co-eds in Madison."

A 19-year-old girl, Peg Seeke, was last seen leaving her dormitory and the next day she was found in a cemetery, strangled and shot in the head twice with a .22-caliber pistol. Her skirt was up around her waist and her tights pulled down around her knees, yet she had not been sexually assaulted. Peg had been killed at a location different from where she was dumped at the cemetery. Her nearly nude body had been posed, laying spread eagle.

The first girl to disappear was a freshman at Edgewood College. She had been savagely beaten and stabbed in the chest multiple times and left along a dirt road near a dairy farm. Like the other victims, she had been killed in another location and dumped at the rural location. The police were questioning the locals to see if they had seen any suspicious vehicles in the area of the body. They suspected the killer or killers returned and moved the decomposing corpse at least two times.

Mark read and reread the articles. As he finished the last he said aloud, "John Norman Collins! My god, it's John Norman Collins all over again."

John Norman Collins, also known as the Co-Ed Killer, was a serial killer who preyed on young women in the Ann Arbor and Ypsilanti area of Michigan between 1967 and 1969. Collins was suspected in the deaths of seven girls between the ages of 13 and 21, six in Michigan and one in California. Although he was only convicted in the murder of his last victim, evidence in the other cases pointed directly to Collins being the perpetrator.

In 1970, Collins was convicted in the murder of his last victim and sentenced to life in prison without the possibility of parole. He was sent to the maximum-security prison in Marquette, Michigan where he remains.

Mark read the chapter on John Norman Collins in Kadar's *Rampage* book and pulled Kadar's first book about the subject off the shelf, *Great Lakes Serial Killers*. Collins was summarized in the *Rampage* book because a full chapter in the first book was devoted to the Co-Ed Killer.

Mark thought, "I definitely see a parallel between these Madison murders and the Collins murders in Michigan." Mark opened his notebook and drew the horizontal and vertical lines of another "Grid of Death" as he began to call them. He wrote notes and made entries on the grid; college town, co-eds, murdered and disposed of in a rural area, posed, violent murders, stabbing, severe beatings. "Oh, these are definitely copycat murders of the murders attributed to John Norman Collins. I've got to call Kadar."

Chapter 30

Mark was in the basement changing the flush mechanism in the old toilet when his cell phone rang upstairs in the kitchen. Sherry picked it up, looked at the caller ID but it read unknown caller. She pressed the accept button and said "Hello?"

"Hello, is Mark there?"

"Yes, I'll go get him. Whom shall I tell him is calling?" she said more out of curiosity than a need to tell Mark who it was.

"This is Eric Holms."

"Okay. Mark is in the basement. It will take a minute.

Eric listened as Sherry walked down the stairs and yelled, "Mark. Telephone." He heard a distant voice answer, "Who is it? I'm up to my elbows in a toilet tank. Tell them I'll call them back."

Sherry said, "It's some guy named Eric Gnomes or Roams or something. If it's a sales call I can just hang up." Eric heard Mark reply, "Gnomes. I don't know anyone by the name Gnomes.'

Mark got up off his knees, wiped his hands on his pants and took the phone. "Hello, this is Mark."

"Hey Mark, this is Eric Holms, Skip Kadar's friend. We met at the mall in Bay City."

"Oh, hi Eric. What can I do for you?" Mark asked wondering why he would be calling.

"I was just talking to Skip and he told me you called him yesterday with another one of your killer theories. Something about a serial killer murdering college girls at the University of Wisconsin like Collins did at U of M and Eastern Michigan."

Mark was walking up the stairs as he responded. "Yeah, it seems some college girls were found dead in Madison and their deaths closely follow the murders of John Norman Collins forty some years ago." Mark began to sit on the couch to look up the Grid of Death for the murders, but Sherry said "Mark!" and shook her head "no" pointing to his butt. His jeans were filthy from sitting on the floor by the toilet and as she told him many times, "You guys have trouble aiming your little squirt guns."

Mark gave her a dirty look, found the grid and walked to the kitchen. "I was just reading the Milwaukee Journal because the Internet was out and came across a story of a girl being found murdered and left in a rural area outside of Madison." Mark took a beer from the fridge and poured it in a tall glass with the imprint of the Ore Dock Brewing Company as he was telling Eric of the similarities between the murders of John Norman Collins and the University of Wisconsin murders.

"Mark," Eric interrupted. "Listen, I thought Skip made it clear that we don't support your theory. He and I discussed it at length and we decided that you have found some stories and molded the facts to fit your bullshit theory."

"But, Eric, one of the girls in Wisconsin was beaten and murdered in the same manner as one of the Collins victims; she was even dumped in a rural area just like ..."

Eric didn't wait for Mark to finish. "Mark, Skip and I agree that your theory is bullshit and we suspect that you might be suffering from some mental problem. We even wondered if you are not the one who is doing all this killing just to prove your point," his voice increasing in anger.

"What?" Mark said not believing what he was hearing. "I haven't molded the facts to suit my theory, I gave you and Skip the facts as I found them and they seem to indicate that there is someone running around the country killing people like it was done in Kadar's book."

"Listen asshole, we don't need or want you're fucking help, and don't contact Skip again," Eric's yelled.

Mark said, "I don't need to take this from you. I'll give Skip a call."

Eric practically screamed in the phone, "I'm speaking for Skip and I'm telling you that we don't want to hear from you anymore. Your ideas are bullshit and we think you are fucking nuts! If you try to contact Skip again we are going to the police to file a restraining order against you!" Then he hung up.

Mark looked at his phone and said, "And he thinks I'm the fucking nut?"

"What was all that about?" Sherry asked.

"Remember I told you about that guy who the author brought along to our meeting? Well, that was him and he was all pissed off and was yelling at me to leave Kadar alone."

"Why?"

"I'm not sure," Mark answered. "It's almost like he is jealous or something. He even said that if I call Kadar again, they would file a restraining order against me."

"You're kidding me?" Sherry asked.

"No, and he said I was fucking nuts," Mark said draining the last of his beer.

Sherry thought for a minute and said, "Well, I can't argue with him on that point. I've been telling you that you're fucking nuts for years."

Chapter 31

Jorge López-Famosa jumped down off the truck, walked to the rear and picked up the garbage can, tossed the contents in the collection hopper just as he had done every weekday morning for the last eleven years. The sun was just rising over the ocean in the east and a salty breeze was blowing across US 1. Jorge hated getting up so early but the job paid well and he had to support his family. He usually got up at 3:20 am, drove to the garage where the collection trucks were maintained and then drove from Homestead down to the Florida Keys where he would pick up the trash from the million dollar homes lining the ocean in Islamorada.

Some of his co-workers didn't have to get up so early, they had routes in Homestead or Florida City or drove transfer trucks, but Jorge liked the Islamorada run. He had to drive for an hour before he started his route but it gave him time to relax, drink a coffee and eat a donut while he drove down US 1 along the 18-mile stretch into Key Largo in the Florida Keys.

Jorge decided long ago that he could be depressed and embarrassed picking up the garbage and cast offs of the rich or he could just live with it and be thankful he had a job. He had many cousins in Cuba that would have killed to make the kind of money he made. His monthly check was almost equal to their annual salary.

After driving down the congested US 1 through Key Largo with cars of vacationers creeping along at less than the speed limit looking around and taking pictures and the locals passing on the right to get to where they needed to be, he continued down the Overseas Highway until he drove across the Tavernier Creek Bridge and into Islamorada, "The Purple Isle." Jorge turned onto Old US 1 and began making stops at the gated homes along the ocean. He jumped from the cab of his truck and quickly walked to the rear, emptied the cans into the hopper, returned the cans to the curb and moved on to the next house.

Every so many stops he would push the switch activating the compression mechanism of the truck. The truck's engine would rev as the hydraulic arms extended, causing the tailgate ram to compress the bags of garbage in the front of the truck, the retainer plate would lower holding the trash in the forward compartment, making more room in the loading hopper. Jorge continued on his route, filling the hopper and compressing it in the forward portion of the truck.

Jorge pulled up to a gated drive so thick with manicured landscaping that the house wasn't visible from the road. He could only dream of the opulence that was beyond the gate, the luxury, and the money it cost to live such a life. At the curb stood two gray plastic cans and a black bag The bag Jorge thought was unusual, this house always put their refuse in cans, and he knew they had at least two more cans they could have used. Jorge dumped the cans in the hopper then threw in the bag. He returned the empty cans to the side of the road and secured the tops on them. The people who lived there were very proper so Jorge always left the cans neatly placed at the curb.

Jorge returned to the truck and pushed the red button activating the tailgate ram. The engine revved as the retainer plate slowly rose and the ram arm gradually lowered and moved forward, compressing the contents of the cans and the black bag. Jorge could hear the sound of cardboard boxes compressing, plastic bags bursting and glass breaking. The retainer plate lowered, keeping the compressed trash from falling back into the loading hopper and at the end of the compression stroke the ram slowly retuned to the up position. Jorge drove on to the next house, picked up a trashcan and carried it to the truck but before he threw it in, he noticed something caught by the lower edge of the retainer plate.

Jorge started to gag, then vomited on the road. Over a decade of breathing in the most vile odors and the sight of rancid decaying food had never caused him to vomit but what he saw was no match for his stomach. Caught under the retainer plate was a hand, a human hand. The little finger was crushed and the ring finger was distorted. The hand was attached to a wrist and forearm. If the arm was attached to a body Jorge couldn't tell; the heavy steel retainer plate was blocking the rest of the macabre sight.

~ ~ ~

The sheriff's department had Jorge follow them to a county facility in the Keys where he emptied the contents of his truck on the concrete floor of a garage. Police dressed in HAZMAT uniforms and breathing through respirators combed through the trash looking for more body parts. The arm Jorge found was lying on a table along with a leg and what appeared to be part of a rib cage. The body parts were found in various non-descript black plastic trash bags in Jorge's truck. Without knowing, Jorge had picked up at least three bags of human remains.

Another collection truck completed Jorge's route and was waiting on the blacktop approach to the garage to dump its contents for the investigators to sort through. The lead crime scene investigator urged his team to do a thorough job but a fast job of opening bags that weren't already opened and picking through the trash. He reminded them that the next truck was waiting and the contents were getting riper the longer it baked in the hot Florida sun.

The sheriff's department alerted other sanitation trucks throughout the Keys that human remains had been found in garbage bags and to be on the lookout for anything suspicious; there could be more.

Detective Scherman and a crime scene investigator that had been dispatched from the mainland were looking over the body parts. The detective said, with a handkerchief held to his nose, "Looks like they were cut off."

"Yeah, someone used a saw of some type to cut the limbs from the body and to cut up the torso." He leaned forward and flipped some strands of flesh dangling from the upper arm with a latex covered finger. "See it's a jagged cut, nothing surgical like a knife would leave. A saw was used, maybe a chain saw."

"Can you get prints from the hand?"

"Already done and sent, and we'll run DNA too," the investigator replied, then offered an opinion. "If I had to make a guess right now, I would say the victim did not die of natural causes."

The detective looked down at the arm, leg and rib cage and said, "No shit!"

A female voice muffled by a respirator yelled, "We have another bag! Looks like a right arm."

The investigator and the detective looked at the arm on the table, the detective said, "Wait, this is a right arm. There are two bodies."

The CSI responded, "At least."

~ ~ ~

"Picking up dog shit in a bag is gross. Why can't we just let it lie like we do at home. Hell, it will decay and be gone in a few days, or sooner if it rains," the man wearing a gray tee shirt with faded red letters reading Ohio State Athletic Department said.

"Because it's on someone else's property and it's the courteous thing to do. Here you take Fyfe's leash and I'll pick it up," his wife said with disgust, tired of fighting with her husband.

"I'll do it!" he said as he opened the bright pink bag and reached down, keeping his head a full arm's length away from the three little turds. "God, I hate the feeling of warm shit in my hand," he said as he quickly tied the top of the bag shut. "Now I suppose you expect me to carry a pink bag of shit around until we get back to the condo."

"There's a trash bag up there by that gate, put Fyfe's pooh in there."

The man walked to the black plastic bag, unwound the twist tie, held his breath, knowing his sensitive stomach, and opened the bag. "Fuck!" he yelled, dropped the bag of Fyfe shit and ran from the trash bag.

"What's wrong with you?" his wife asked picking up Fyfe's pretty pink bag of poop.

"Don't come here! Don't throw that in the bag!" he told her from twenty feet away, gagging on the words.

She and Fyfe slowly walked towards her husband, "What's wrong..." He had his phone to his ear and a palm up telling her to be quiet."

~ ~ ~

"We have some more parts," the Monroe County coroner told Detective Scherman. "A couple from Ohio taking their dog out for a walk found a severed head in a trash bag down on Big Pine Key."

The murderer must have killed his victims then disposed of their bodies in trash bags from Key West to Key Largo," Scherman said. "I'm sure the rest of the body parts are rotting in the garbage dump buried beneath ten feet of trash by now."

Through finger prints and DNA the police determined the victims were James Bonet and Philip Weismann. Bonet lived in Key West and was a waiter at an upscale restaurant. A few years ago he had a couple of arrests for male prostitution. Weismann was vacationing with a couple of guys in Key West from Chicago and was reported to be frequenting gay bars. His friends said they didn't see him hook up with anyone but figured he had when he didn't come back to their motel. The head found on Big Pine Key was Bonet's.

Since land is scarce in the Keys, there is not a permanent dumpsite. The collection trucks pick up the garbage and take it to one of three transfer sites throughout the string of islands. From there it is trucked out of the Keys in transfer trucks to a permanent disposal site on the Florida mainland. The Sheriff's department stopped all transfer trucks and deputies wearing respirators searched the transfer sites with cadaver dogs. Three more bags were found containing parts of James Bonet and Philip Weismann; a forearm, a thigh, entrails and a buttocks.

Detective Scherman called his wife. "Sue, I won't be home any time soon. I have to go to Key West for a few days. No, don't worry about me eating; I lost my appetite."

Chapter 32

Winter in Michigan's Upper Peninsula is only for the hardiest of souls. The snow usually comes early and stays late. This year the first snowstorm blew in from the north and dumped eight inches of the white stuff in October and it will probably be the last snow to melt in May. Mark enjoyed the first snow of the year, everything so white and clean, the air so fresh and invigorating but his enthusiasm for winter went downhill from there. He shoveled the back porch and steps and a path to the garage then went to the lakeside and shoveled a small section of the deck by the door, the steps, and a five foot by five foot square down to bare grass. "Here's your piss and poop area you little flea bag," Mark mumbled aloud to the dog.

That was all Mark needed to shovel because Jake, the young guy down the road who plowed for Mark, would do the rest. Jake had bought a new diesel truck, at least a truck new to him, and invested in big wide tires with new shiny rims and dressed it out with every piece of aftermarket chrome he could find. He took on plow jobs to pay off his baby.

He would start plowing at the county road and work his way along Sherry and Mark's 1/8-mile drive, pushing the snow to the sides. When he got to the cottage, Jake with the unabashed exuberance of youth would back up and take a running start and smash into snow pushing it well off the drive leaving room for the rest of winter's snow to pile up, then back up and do it again and again making a huge snow mountain west of the driveway.

Mark left the shovel at the back door, knowing he would need it again, and walked in the rear entrance into the laundry room. He stomped his feet knocking the snow from his boots as he took off his gloves. He leaned on the washer bouncing around on the spin cycle and used his right foot to peel off his left boot. "I hope there is still some coffee left!" Mark yelled to Sherry. "I froze my ass off shoveling a spot for your hairball to pee."

Sherry walked into the laundry room with a mug of coffee in one hand and the dog in the other. From the mug, vapors of steam rose from the hot black liquid and a snarly look of disdain came from the dog. "Awww, you're so good to our little princess." She scratched the dog behind the ears and gave it several kisses on the head saying, "See how nice daddy is to you. Daddy loves his little girl." Mark rolled his eyes in disgust and set the coffee down and placed his cold hands on either side of Sherry's face and said, "And I love you, too."

"Get your cold hands off of me," Sherry yelled.

Mark lowered his hands to the bottom of her sweatshirt and tried to get his hands to the warm of her flesh below but she jumped back, pushing his hands away with her free hand.

"But, Sweetie, I'm cold and all I want is for your hot body to warm me up."

Sherry, with the dog in her arms, backed out of the laundry room saying, "Come on, you pervert, I've got a breakfast casserole in the oven and it's almost ready."

After breakfast and another failed attempt to get his hands under Sherry's sweatshirt where he was pretty sure he would find she wasn't wearing a bra, Mark settled on the couch in front of the computer. He had already checked the online newspapers when he got up at 5:17 and didn't find anything of interest so he was just aimlessly surfing around the Internet until his phone rang.

"Hello?" He answered his phone. "Yes, this is Mark." Mark listened. "Oh, hello", Mark said confused. It was Kadar. He thought, "But Eric said no contact or they would get a restraining order but now he is calling me."

Sherry looked at her husband and silently asked, "Who is it?"

Mark wrote on the notebook in front of him, "Kadar, author of *Rampage*." Sherry shook her head up and down with a perplexed look, knowing the history.

"Mark did you hear about the bodies found in the Florida Keys?" Kadar asked. Not waiting for a response he proceeded to tell him what he had heard. "Eric, my friend you met in Bay City, heard about body parts being found in garbage bags throughout the Keys. I did some research and couldn't find any information but it seems someone killed a couple of guys, chopped them up and stuffed the pieces in garbage bags and left them at the curb along US 1. It sounds remarkably like the chapter in *Rampage* about Bob Berdella. He was a serial killer from Kansas City, Missouri who murdered other gay men then cut them into pieces with a chain saw and disposed of them by putting them in trash bags to be picked up by the garbage truck. Do you think this could be another copycat murder?"

"Skip, I thought you said my theory was a bunch of bullshit and not to bother you anymore with it?"

"I didn't say that. I said I was skeptic, it was a lot of circumstantial evidence and possibly coincidence but not bullshit. I have been giving it a lot of thought. Anyway, about the body parts in the Keys..." he said bringing the conversation back to the reason he called. "Have you read or heard anything about it?"

"No, I haven't heard anything about it." Mark answered as he was scribbling in his notebook. "How did you hear about it?"

"Eric was down in the Keys when the bodies were found. There wasn't much in the newspapers but he heard from a guy at the motel where he was staying that two bodies were found chopped up and stuffed in garbage bags. And the guys were gay, just like in the Bob Berdella chapter from my book."

Mark thought, "Oh Eric said" and answered, "I'll have to re-read the chapter but it's similarities like this that got me to look deeper into the murders in your book. What have you found online about the murders?" Mark did a quick Google search for Florida Keys murders.

Kadar answered, "I haven't been able to find anything about body parts being found in the garbage. Like I said, Eric was down there and heard about it from a guy who worked at the motel where he was staying."

"Hey, I have another call coming in. Check it out and get back to me," Kadar said.

Mark said, "But, wait, I want to talk to you..." Kadar had hung up. Mark wanted to talk him about the phone call he received from Eric.

Chapter 33

"**M**an, I am really confused. First Kadar is excited about the comparison of murders, then he thinks it's a bunch of coincidences, then when I call him about the Madison murders he gets excited again, then Eric calls and tells me I'm a fucking nut and to never call again, Now Kadar calls with information about a possible copycat killing that Eric told him about. Eric will probably call next yelling and screaming at me for trying to steal his friend."

Sherry handed Mark a cup of coffee and said, "It has been snowing all morning and the princess needs to go out but the snow is too deep in her pee pee and poopy field."

Mark thought, "I like how Sherry didn't tell me to go out and shovel for the furry rodent; she was just making a statement that the snow in the poop field was too deep. She was letting me come to the conclusion that I had better go out and shovel for the fuzzy little shit machine."

~ ~ ~

By the time Mark had finished his shoveling, he could hear Jake plowing down at the county road. It would be 5 minutes or so before he appeared at the cottage.

With his feet out of boots and being warmed in his slippers, and his stomach being warmed with each sip of his Manhattan, Mark watched out the back window as Jake plowed the snow from the drive. As he always did, Jake backed up much further than necessary, almost into the woods, and took a run into the snow and smashed into it sending a cloud of white into the air.

Sherry walked up next to Mark and put her arm around his waist saying, "Thank you for shoveling for the princess. Hey, look the snow is green under Jake's truck. Is he leaking something?"

"No, it looks like Jake installed some L.E.D. lights under the truck to reflect off the snow."

They watched as Jake backed up, he lowered the plow, revved the engine, sending a thick cloud of black smoke from the vertical exhaust pipes, then raced forward into the pile of snow shoving it into the snow mound next to the driveway.

"It's kind of pretty," Sherry said. "Everything is white and the truck casts off neon green highlights."

"And don't forget about the haze of black diesel exhaust hanging in the air," Mark added.

~ ~ ~

After dinner, Sherry and Mark settled in the living room. The fireplace cast a warm yellowish light on the walls and warmed the room with its dry heat. Mark turned on the floodlights on the lakeside of the house so they could watch the snow falling; big flakes, great big flakes that accumulated quickly. Sherry and the dog sat in the recliner as she always did and Mark sat on the couch absorbed in something on the computer.

"I miss television," Sherry said. "Most of the time it doesn't bother me that we don't have television but tonight it does. I feel like watching something. Mark do you want to watch a movie? You could run down to the little store and rent one or you can set up that Kufu or Ruku thing and we can watch something on Netflix. What do you think? It's time we do something different than you playing on the computer and me playing scrabble against the iPad."

Mark needed a break from the computer anyway. "Okay, but I get to choose," he told his wife.

"Oh, no you don't. You picked one out last time and we ended up watching that awful movie about college kids trapped on a deserted island with zombie gorillas chasing them."

"Yeah, it was pretty bad but the acting was superb," Mark said with a smirk.

Sherry looked at her husband and said, "You just liked it because the girls were running through the jungle topless."

~ ~ ~

"Will it ever quit snowing?" Sherry asked looking out the wall of glass at the ice forming on the lake. "There's the eagle. He's on this side of the lake. He must sense something to eat. He is circling above us."

Mark got up and walked to the door saying to the dog, "Come on eagle bait, let's go outside."

"Mark!" Sherry yelled.

He looked at his wife with a smirk then returned to the couch and computer. Mark was doing some research on the effects of meth when his cell rang.

"Hello?" Mark said then held the phone away from his ear a bit because Eric was screaming on the other end.

"Hey shit face, what the fuck are you trying to do? I told you to stay away from Skip. I warned you and you had to keep butting in where you're not wanted. Well, this is your final warning; stay away from Skip or else!"

During his years with the Free Press Mark had received calls like this before and couldn't resist, "Or else what?"

"Listen fuckwad, you don't know who you're fuckin with. I was Special Forces and I can kill you in a hundred different ways. Don't fuck with me! And leave Skip alone. If there is any connection between your fucked up theory and his books, we will take care of it. Understand? Now keep the fuck out of our business!" The phone went dead.

~ ~ ~

Mark walked to the kitchen, poured two inches of Jameson's in a glass and threw it back, then poured three more and walked to the living room. He stood by the fireplace, warming his backside and told Sherry about his conversation.

"You have to call the police," Sherry told her husband.

"Yes I may but I want to think this through first. He may be a hot head and flies off the handle when he doesn't get his way then regrets it the next day. Maybe he suffers from PTSD? I mean he is a guy with a responsible job and I think he is married or was married."

Sherry gave Mark a worried look and said, "Maybe he killed her."

Chapter 34

Before they went to bed that night, Mark made sure all the doors and windows were locked. He double checked the basement at Sherry's insistence and left all of the exterior lights on. Sherry moved over in the bed until she was against Mark. She even moved the dog to the foot of the bed so she could be as close to Mark as possible.

Mark pulled her close, knowing she was afraid. He lay awake for a while thinking about the phone call, assessing it, trying to determine how serious Eric was. "What did he mean by, if there is any connection between my fucked up theory and Kadar's books that they would take care of it. Does Eric want Kadar to be the one to discover it and make it public? Could Eric be responsible for the murders?"

Somewhere after 1:00 am while he lay with Sherry cuddled at his side, Mark's reality drifted to dreams. He dreamt of standing at the wall of windows facing the lake, the eagle circling overhead, the fox walking along the shore and an army landing craft on the lake preparing to make an amphibious assault on his beach. Mark watched in horror as Eric stood at the bow in true Sylvester Stallone, Rambo style; with an automatic weapon in his hands, a pistol on his waist, a bandolier of ammunition across his chest and a knife clenched between his teeth.

As the boat reached the shore and the front lowered to discharge its cargo of troops and a tank, Mark awoke with a start. Realizing he was dreaming, Mark looked to see if he had awakened Sherry or the dog. Sherry, still asleep, rolled on her side. The dog gave Mark a look of disgust. He took a deep breath, laughed at himself and lay back down. "Man, 5:17 is going to come early. Maybe I'll sleep in."

He had trouble falling back to sleep. Mark kept thinking about Eric and his outburst and threats. "I have to call Kadar tomorrow and get things straightened out," He decided. "If they want to break the news of the murders, fine, go for it." The next thing Mark noticed was a disgusting odor, a really foul stench. He lay there smelling the stink when he noticed a large black eye staring at him. As he looked at the eye, wishing he could squeeze his nostrils closed, he heard a noise that sounded like someone sniffing, but louder and then a snort. He turned his head away from the eye and saw a large sow; she must have weighed close to 500 pounds standing in the mud of the pen. She was gnawing on something. Another pig waddled over to it and tried to take its meal, but the first pig grunted and snorted in disapproval and picked up her dinner and walked away. It was an arm, a human arm, from the elbow to the hand, the fingers were missing but it was an arm. Mark could see the palm and noticed a scar in the fleshy part below the thumb. "Someone must have cut themselves with a utility knife like I did," Mark thought.

Mark turned his head back to the big black eye and realized it was a hog, a big hog and beyond the hog another pig was standing by his foot chewing something. Mark looked down the length of his body, noticed he was nude and that his left arm was missing and several of his toes on his right foot were gone. The big black eye was sniffing at his stomach which was ripped open and there was blood on its snout.

"No!" Mark yelled. He realized the pigs were devouring him! He wasn't a bystander watching this macabre scene; he was a participant, the main course. "I've got to wake up," Mark thought. "This is the nightmare; I've got to wake up." Mark watched as the hog at his feet bit and chewed part of his left foot and the big beast next to him lowered its head into the gaping hole of Mark's stomach and came out with a large section of bloody intestine. "No!" he screamed at the animal, "No!" Mark felt something on his shoulder. He instinctively tried to swat the pig away but his arm was missing. He thrashed from side to side trying to scare the pigs away before they devoured him; he wanted Sherry to have something to bury.

Mark felt the movement on his shoulder as the pig ripped a large piece of his flesh away and in the distance he heard Sherry yelling his name. "Oh God, she's not watching this is she? Are they making her watch the pigs ripping me apart and eating me bit by bit until they have consumed every inch of my body?"

"Mark!" he heard her scream.

"Run! Sherry run away, don't watch!"

"Mark!" he heard again. "Wake up, it's a nightmare. You're alright, everything is okay."

Mark opened his eyes, looked confused at his wife trying to make sense of the pigs, wondering why she was there, wondering why she was yelling at him. He raised his left arm, looked at the scar below his thumb, rubbed a hand over his stomach then his reality overcame his subconscious and he looked at Sherry.

"Sorry," Mark said embarrassed. "Go back to sleep. I'm alright. I'm going to go downstairs to calm down. I'm sorry, go back to sleep."

Mark got out of bed, grabbed the flashlight from his bedside stand and his robe, then went down the stairs, turning on the fireplace and looking around the house for assassins, butchers, murderers and pigs.

Mark opened his eyes and checked the wall clock. In the illumination of the fire he read 5:17. "I'm not getting up yet. Shit, I have gotten less than four hours of sleep." Mark rolled on his side, the couch not offering too much room, pulled up the afghan Sherry's sister knitted or crocheted or bought or something, put a throw pillow over his head and thankfully fell asleep.

~ ~ ~

Mark heard the dog bark. He pulled the pillow off his head and looked at the clock. It was 8:35. "Wow, that felt good. That was the most sound sleep I had all night." The dog barked again.

Mark looked at the door and the dog was sitting there demanding that Mark get up and let her out. As he threw the afghan off, Mark could smell coffee. Sherry was up and had made coffee. He looked around the room and noticed the bathroom door was closed. The dog barked again. "Okay, okay, you furry fart, let's go outside. Mark looked for signs of the fox or the eagle but all he saw was snow. It was snowing when he went to bed and it was still snowing. Mark opened the door for the mutt. The dog took a look out at the snow and hesitated, with Mark's foot gentlly urging her from behind, she went out.

The dog quickly did its business and ran to the door and barked for Mark to let her in. Between the big flakes falling and the six or so inches of snow that fell last night, the pooch was covered in snow. The princess walked in, stopped by Mark and shook as if she intentionally wanted to get snow on his bare feet. "Thanks a lot, you little piss bucket." Mark was pretty sure the dog was smiling as she walked away to stand guard at the bathroom door.

Chapter 35

Armed with a hot cup of coffee, his trusty notebook and pencil, Mark sat on the couch and wrote down his thoughts of what he wanted to talk to Kadar about. Eric was out of control and Mark needed to tell Kadar that Eric was threatening him.

Sherry asked, "Are you going to call that author guy and tell him what a strange person his friend is?"

Mark smiled and said, "That's an understatement. He's a fucking nutcase." Mark wrote something in his notebook. "I decided I'm going to compose an email and send it to Kadar. I do better conveying my thoughts on paper. And maybe an email won't piss off Eric as much if I don't actually talk to Skip."

Mark had a few notes, but not enough to start typing the text of an email. He alternately wrote, thought, sipped coffee and stared out the window at the lake for close to twenty minutes. "How do I tell a guy his good friend is a raving lunatic that threatened to kill me if I didn't stay away from him?"

Mark scribbled in the notebook Eric's exact words, "I was Special Forces and I can kill you in a hundred different ways." Mark thought, "Was that a direct threat on my life or simply the ravings of a crazy person?" Mark looked back out at the lake and wondered, "What brought about his anger? Does he think I'm trying to butt into his friendship with Kadar, does he think I'm going to try to take publicity away from the *Rampage* book for my own book, a book that may never be written? Hell, for all I know Eric has romantic feelings for the author and he is jealous of me taking up his time?"

He thought, "This isn't the first time I have been threatened; in my career of chasing murderers I have pissed off some really nasty people. Some people who had already killed and wouldn't think twice about killing again. I really don't think Eric falls in that category. I think he is a bully, a bully that can't verbalize his thoughts very well and instead lashes out at people when he can't make his point."

Mark watched light snow flurries gently falling. A duck was waddling across the ice near shore. He watched a variety of birds lunching at the birdfeeder he filled yesterday and now it was more than half gone. Despite the problem with "Eric the Nut", Mark was enjoying the peacefulness and tranquility the winter day offered.

"Mark," Sherry said bringing him back to reality, "Mark, don't forget you need to shovel the sidewalk and porch."

"Yeah," Mark said, but thought, "She says the sidewalk and porch but what she really means is for me to shovel the pee and shit field for the poopy pooch." "Okay, I'll go do it now. I need a break from composing this email anyway."

Mark pulled on his wool socks, insulated jeans, a flannel shirt over his insulated undershirt, his down coat, Sorel boots, and a Stormy Kromer to warm his head.

"Mark," Sherry yelled from the loft where she was making the bed, "I can hear Jake's truck down by the road, you better hurry up. You don't want to be out back when Jake is plowing or he'll plow you into the snow mountain he's making next to the driveway."

"Nope, don't want to become part of Mt. Jacob," Mark yelled up to the loft. The dog, sitting with its head between the spindles of the railing, looked at Mark as if it were saying, "Get out there and shovel, I have to poop and I don't want to put my butt in the snow!"

Mark noticed the new snow was about five inches deep, light and fluffy. "At least it's not a heart attack snow; that heavy wet stuff can kill a guy," he thought. He listened as Jake's truck got closer. He had the back porch and sidewalk shoveled and moved to the lakeside deck, steps and the poop field. "This is going to stink when it thaws," Mark thought as he shoveled the snow and previously deposited frozen turds into a small pile.

He finished in time to watch Jake plow the drive; it was always entertaining. Jake would slowly back up as far as he could, the heavy steel plow lowered to the ground, the lead edge cutting into the turf Mark worked so hard to grow. Jake revved the engine and black plumes of smoke poured from the two exhaust pipes Jake had installed vertically on either side of the truck's cab like a mini semi-truck. He slammed his truck into gear and floored it. With all four wheels driving, the truck surged forward much faster than necessary for the light fluffy accumulation and cleared an eight foot wide path. At a speed much faster than necessary, Jake smashed into the mountain, pushing and condensing the new layer of snow up on Mt. Jacob, then backed up to clear another swath.

Mark went inside and stood with Sherry watching the kid plow. "He enjoys this entirely too much," Sherry said.

"That's for sure," Mark said as he peeled off his winter wear, gloves, coat, hat and boots and walked into the living room to stand in front of the fireplace to chase away the chill. He said to Sherry, "It's the unbridled freedom of youth. He is completely unaware of the damage he is doing to his truck. He just enjoys the thrill of the moment. Someday he will grow up but until then he is having fun."

Sherry, still at the back door watching Jake plowing the driveway said, "Mark, I was thinking that if we enjoy watching Jake plow our drive so much that we look forward to the next snow storm, then we really need to get away from here next winter. I think we may have cabin fever."

Mark looked at the laptop and remembered he had to write Kadar about Eric. Not that he forgot that Eric had threatened him but shoveling and watching Jake had pushed the email to the back of his gray matter. "I had better get back at it."

Mark picked up the notebook and re-read his notes. He sat transfixed on the paper before him, tapping the pencil's eraser against his cheek as he thought and was startled when his cell phone rang.

"Hello?" Mark said.

Chapter 36

"**M**ark!" the author said excitedly into the phone. "Did you read the newspapers today? The murders in the Keys are all over the headlines."

"No," Mark said. He was so upset by Eric's call and preoccupied with writing an email to Kadar that he didn't follow his normal routine and peruse the news. "No, I didn't."

"The rumors were flying down in Key West about gays being murdered, about some psychopath cutting up their bodies in little pieces and the police not doing anything about it," Kadar continued. "They were, of course, but they were trying to keep it quiet because a killer running around paradise killing people, chopping them up into little pieces and sticking their body parts in trash bags isn't good for tourism."

"Last weekend, I guess a bunch of guys at one of the more well-known gay bars on Duval Street got all riled up at the lack of information and decided to march down Duval in a noisy drunken protest. Along the way people in other bars, both gay and straight, joined in the impromptu parade and a group of a few hundred protesting drunks interrupted the sunset celebration at Mallory Square. Probably half of them didn't know what they were protesting, but I guess the street performers got pissed off because it interrupted their performances and they only work for tips, you know. So it was messing with their livelihood. They started yelling at the protesting drunks and the next thing you know a drunken brawl broke out. All the families, moms, dads and kids and the ma's and pa's from Podunk, Iowa went running scared and screaming from Mallory Square. Not the kind of publicity Key West wants getting out and scaring away the families and senior citizens who spend generously."

The author continued to tell Mark what he knew. "The publicity of an invasion of Mallory Square by hundreds of drunks was probably worse than if the police had just been open about the crime and made periodic press releases in the first place. Anyway, the result is that the police and sheriff's department came out with a statement about the murders. It's nothing we didn't already know but it confirms what Eric had told me."

"Hey Skip!" Mark interrupted, "I have to talk to you about Eric."

"Yeah, what's up?"

Mark didn't want to do this verbally but the opportunity presented itself and he had to take it. "He called me ranting and swearing to leave you alone. That you and he don't subscribe to the theory of a copycat murderer and that you were going to call the police and get a restraining order against me if I contacted you again."

"Oh, he can be a hot head at times. Just ignore him. I'll talk to him. By the way, at first I didn't believe that someone was copying the serial killers in my book but now I'm not so sure. This Key West stuff and the murders in Wisconsin are changing my mind."

Mark listened and finally interrupted, "But, the last time Eric called he said if I didn't leave you alone he would kill me! He told me he was in the Army Special Forces and knew a hundred ways to kill a man."

"Mark, I am sorry. I know Eric thinks your theory is a bunch of bullshit and he suggested I distance myself from you but I had no idea he was calling and threatening you. I know he has been talking to a counselor at the VA."

"I've known Eric for most of my life, we went to high school together and I've never known him to be violent. I mean he got into a couple of fights in high school and he was in Special Forces and he said he did some not so pleasant things in Iraq, but as a civilian I've only known him to be a nice guy. I'll talk to him. I enjoy talking with you about the theory. I find it intriguing. Heck, maybe it will be a good novel for you to write. Never mind about Eric. He won't bother you anymore."

"Thanks Skip. I didn't think he would actually show up at my house and sneak up behind me and wrap a garrote around my neck or anything but being threatened is a bit disconcerting.

The two men talked more about the Keys murders and the deaths of the co-eds in Wisconsin and their similarities to the *Rampage* book. They promised to stay in touch and to share any and all information. Kadar assured Mark again that he would talk to Eric as soon as he could and get that all straightened out.

The rest of the day Sherry did laundry, checked Facebook, played Sudoku, made lunch, and checked Facebook again. Both Sherry and Mark agreed that retirement was great. You could pretty well do what you want when you want, and Mark was pretty sure Sherry and the dog had taken a nap when she was up making the bed, at least they took an awfully long time to make the bed. Mark had to agree that the mid-day nap was one of the better benefits of retirement.

It was parmesan encrusted whitefish night at the Jack Pine, their standing date night. Mark wanted to go out but he had to convince Sherry that they needed to get out or they would go crazy and start acting like Jack Nicholson in the movie *The Shining*. Mark thought, "Probably not the best analogy considering they had a crazy person threatening to kill him but it worked and Sherry agreed.

Mark and Sherry got bundled up and ventured out into the snowy evening. As they backed out of the garage, it was lightly snowing and cold, the thermometer read a chilly 14 degrees.

During the eight mile ride home, the car thermometer read 11 degrees and it was still snowing. "We shouldn't get too much snow, it's too cold," Mark said, driving slowly on the snow covered highway with the windshield wipers whisking away the falling snow. "I don't think we are supposed to get too much snow tonight but the prediction for the next week has snow every day."

"Much accumulation?" Sherry asked.

"I think a few inches each day and heavier accumulation later in the week."

Sherry said, "Good, then we will have Jake around to entertain us. You know, I am really getting tired of all this snow. Maybe next winter we should go to Florida and see what the sun looks like. We can go visit your sister for a week and my old friend from college has a place in Boca Raton, we could visit her. Don't you have some friends from the newspaper who retired down there we can visit?"

"I agree after the winter we have had this year we should venture south but I'm not going to spend a month or two mooching on friends around the state. If we go, I want to get a place and stay there. Somewhere I can relax and not entertain or be entertained 24/7. I would like to spend some time down in the Keys. I haven't been there since college."

~ ~ ~

Over a cocktail, cuddled up on the couch, Sherry petted the dog and Mark thought about the day, his talk with Kadar, and how the gay population in Key West took it upon themselves to force the authorities to release information about the murders and mutilation of the two men down there. He also felt confident that Kadar would corral Eric and get him to lay off. Mark turned to Sherry and kissed her on the top of the head. She turned towards him   and   said,   "I   love   you."

Chapter 37

Eric lay on the bed staring at the ceiling in a motel room not much different than the 97 other motel rooms he slept in this year during his business trips around the country.

Eric had some thinking to do, choices to make. He already made one decision; Mark had to die. Now he had to decide on the details, like where, when and how he would kill Mark.

Mark got in the way of his plan. Eric wanted to make Kadar's new serial killer book, *Rampage,* a best seller, and decided to do some unconventional marketing. He thought that since there hadn't been any famous serial killers to capture the attention of the public since John Wayne Gacy, Ted Bundy or Jeffery Dahmer, all active killers in the 1970's, he would need to create interest in a serial killer; one who was roaming the country randomly selecting innocent people to murder. He thought that if the killer only killed in one state or one region like the Midwest, then people on the west or east coast wouldn't fear the killer and wouldn't pay close attention to the deaths. Eric wanted the entire country to live in fear. He wanted to terrorize the entire population of the United States. The more people murdered in various parts of the country the better. And when the connection between the *Rampage* book and the murders was made, the sales of the book would skyrocket. People would not be able to read enough about serial killers. They would buy *Rampage* and all of the 14 other books Kadar had written. Overnight he would become "the author" to read, the man to interview on the talk shows. He would be an instant success, and all because of Eric.

Eric was hoping to somehow alert Kadar to the connection to the murders and let him make the discovery and get all the publicity. Even if the police or FBI made the connection, Kadar would get the attention because the deaths follow his books. Unfortunately, neither the police, FBI nor Kadar noticed the similarities of the crimes and the chapters in *Rampage*; instead, a retired newspaper reporter, living in the sticks, made the discovery.

Eric thought, "And now the reporter was trying to get all the attention. He was going to write a book and get publicity for it by claiming he discovered the copycat killings. Well, that asshole ain't going to take credit for something that's not rightfully his. I murdered those people and if the authorities aren't smart enough to figure out the connection with *Rampage*, then I'll have to arrange Kadar to follow up on the discovery. But for now Mark is in the way so he will have to become my next victim. It's time for the reporter to die."

Eric was a very methodical person and always made plans down to the last detail. It was his attention to detail that made him so successful with the Special Forces. He knew the end result of his mission, he planned how he would accomplish the mission, he anticipated things that could go wrong, he planned contingent courses of action, and if others in his unit didn't follow his strict lead, he took care of them. They were simply collateral damage. He hated relying on other people. He always considered other people to be the weakest part of a plan. He had the utmost control over what he did but he couldn't control the actions of others.

Chapter 38

"Hello? Yes this is Wayne Kadar," the author said into the receiver. "What's your name again?"

"Ms. Johnson, where did you get that information and how did you get my phone number?" Kadar asked the reporter.

"An anonymous tip?" Kadar repeated. Did they call you or write you, how did you get it?" Kadar waited for the answer.

"No, I don't have anything to say at this time. No, Ms. Johnson I don't have a comment. Goodbye Ms. Johnson," the author said as the reporter began another question.

He dialed Eric's cell but he didn't pick up so Kadar left a message; "Eric, did you send an email to a reporter about the possible ties between the murders in my book and the murders that Mark Daniels uncovered? I got a call from a reporter and she was asking a lot of questions. Call me as soon as you get this."

The longer he waited for Eric to call back, the angrier he became. "The only people that know of the similarities are Mark, Eric and I," he thought. "Unless Mark told other people, but Mark was the one that said we should keep it quiet. That leaves Eric. I could see him contacting a reporter as a way to give book sales a boost but after the meeting at the food court, Eric said he thought Mark was delusional and the whole theory was based on coincidences. No, it wouldn't be Eric. It must be Mark who leaked this. He said he was working on a novel; maybe he did it to get some publicity for his book. I'm going to call him."

Pacing across the living room floor, Kadar pressed the Mark Daniels selection in the contact list of his phone. He took a drink of his coffee and continued pacing as the phone on the other end rang. The call went to voice mail. "Dammit," the author silently said and hung up. He didn't want to leave a message; he wanted to talk to Mark in person.

~ ~ ~

Mark was putting the groceries in the back of the car as Sherry talked to Mickie on her cell. He put the frozen food in insulated bags as Sherry instructed but it was 23 degrees out and Mark didn't think thawing would be an issue. "Why is grocery shopping something that is a he and she thing with retirees?" Mark thought. "It seems like all of our retired friends go shopping together. Sherry did just fine doing the shopping by herself before we retired and now she won't go unless I go along too."

He slammed the back hatch and climbed in the driver's side door. Sherry was still talking with Mickie as he pulled into the traffic of US 2 heading back to the cottage. "I mean, I can see Sherry wanting me to unload the groceries when she got home, but why do I have to walk through the aisles pushing the cart while she takes stuff off the shelves and scratches them off her list. And God forbid if I grab some cookies or a bag of Better Made Honey BBQ chips or something. She uses that, "We're on a fixed income" routine. So I tell her to get a job and fix it. Better yet, why am I spending so much time thinking about this when I have a book to think about and murders to solve."

Sherry hung up. "Mickie had to get off. Someone walked into her office." "She says hi. Oh and Mark, you left your cell phone in the drink holder and it dinged while you were loading the car."

161

Mark picked up the phone and looked at the screen; the call came in twenty-three minutes ago. He hit redial.

"Skip, this is Mark Daniels. How are you doing? What? No, I didn't tell anyone. The only people I told are my wife, you and Eric. Well, I did tell the FBI but since they never got back to me I don't think they really care."

"Who called you? Kate who? Did she say how she heard about it? No, I wouldn't tell anyone, I don't even know if I believe it myself."

"Have you checked with Eric? He said the publicity would sell a bunch of books," Mark said. "Maybe he is doing some marketing."

The author replied, "I've got a call in to him but I haven't heard back from him yet. He might be out on the road. He travels a lot for business."

Mark told Sherry about the call and explained that they had all agreed to keep the idea of a copycat murderer under cover until they had either disproved it or had enough evidence to prove it. As far as Mark knew the only people who knew about the similarities were him, Sherry, Kadar and Eric. He knew he had not said anything to a reporter or anyone who would leak it to a reporter. He knew Sherry wouldn't say anything because, first of all, she knew throughout his career to keep quiet about anything he was working on and, secondly, she really didn't care about what he was working on. She only listened to him as a courtesy when he wanted to talk about it. Mark knew she didn't actually pay attention to him.

"That leaves Kadar and Eric," Mark said to himself. "It's possible that they both released the theory to get some PR for the book. They could be in this together, although Kadar seemed genuinely upset that the information had leaked. I'm sure he would enjoy the publicity it would generate for his books, but if this is just a bunch of bullshit then he will come off as just another nutcase, another crazy person screaming conspiracy which could destroy his reputation along with sales of the books. That leaves Eric. And who knows what he would do. He's already proven himself to be a fucking nut."

With groceries put away and the fireplace lit, Mark and Sherry retired to the comfort of the cottage, she in her recliner with the warm body of the little dog warming her legs and he on the couch with a laptop warming his. "I wonder?" Mark said aloud, then thought to himself, "I wonder where else Eric travels? He was in Florida when the two guys were murdered and dismembered; in fact he was in the Florida Keys, right where it happened. I wonder where else he has been when a copycat murder had occurred? How can I find out his schedule? I can't ask the author. He might be in on the murder scheme too." Mark was deep in thought thinking about Eric and Kadar being the murderers when he was interrupted.

"Earth to Mark. Earth to Mark, this is flight control. Where are you?"

"Oh, I was just thinking. Sorry, am I ignoring you?" Mark said to Sherry. "I really hate to interrupt your fantasy, but the princess needs to go out and the snow is too deep. Can you shovel for her? I imagine Jake will be around soon. You don't want to miss the entertainment, do you?"

While Mark was shoveling the porch, steps, deck and frozen little dog turds, Sherry took a phone call. Jake called to apologize that he got called back to the paper mill and couldn't plow until after his shift. He would be there in the evenings except weekends, not too late, he promised, but he would take care of the snow. "Well, he will be plowing in the dark; now the green lights under his truck will really show up," Sherry said. "God, I must be suffering from cabin fever if I'm anticipating seeing Jake plow and seeing his green lights."

Mark decided there was no way he could find out Eric's schedule without asking Kadar. It was a long shot based purely on conjecture. Just because Eric was in the Keys when a murder occurred doesn't mean he was anywhere near the other deaths. If he was a cop on a TV show he would just type a little on a keyboard and Eric's complete travel agenda for the year would pop up on the screen. Then all he would need to do was compare location and dates with the copycat murders. If he was anywhere near a death location within the timeframe of the murders, he would definitely be a suspect. Mark thought, "Unfortunately that is TV and it can't be confused with reality. I guess the only way I can find out Eric's schedule is to ask Kadar."

Mark needed to figure out a way to ask Kadar about Eric's schedule without raising any suspicion. "If Kadar is part of this, I don't want to let them know I suspect them and then they come after me. Or if he isn't part of this, I don't want Kadar to think I'm some crazy person and tell Eric that I suspect he is a raving lunatic, going around the country murdering innocent people. "Eric the Nut" is already not too happy with me and I don't need to piss off a crazy person who may be running around the country murdering people, especially one who has already threatened to kill me."

"Maybe I can call Kadar and slowly steer the conversation around to Eric and what he does and where he does it," Mark thought. "Or I could just come out and ask if Eric is murdering people. No, I better not use the direct approach."

Mark mixed a rum and Coke and sat down to scribble his thoughts in a notebook. The pencil had an eraser but the page Mark was working on had a lot of scratched out sentences, evidence he didn't know how to approach the subject and what to say. "I need to do something else and maybe it will come to me." Mark checked the Detroit News website.

Chapter 39

"**M**ark!" Kadar almost shouted into the phone. "Did you hear about the woman and her child who were killed in Montana? The dead woman was a widow and met a man on an Internet dating service. The guy killed her and her child, buried them in the basement then lived in the house for a couple of days. When neighbors asked he told them the woman was out of town and he was there to watch the house."

"Hi, Skip," Mark said. "No, I didn't see that. When did it happen? Wait a minute. I think I did see that. It was a while ago wasn't it?"

"Yes, it was on September 16th.

Mark was thumbing through the pages in his notebook. "Yeah, here it is. Why?"

"In *Rampage*, there is a chapter about a man who befriended a lonely widow and he ended up killing and burying her and her child in the basement. The Montana woman was killed with her child and they were both buried in her basement. This looks like another copycat murder. And I'm sure of that date because it's my birthday," Kadar said. "Eric heard about the murder and told me about it when he called to wish me happy birthday. He happened to be in Montana when it happened."

It was the opening Mark was looking for. "Skip. I have a question. I hope I don't piss you off by asking but it's something I need to ask. Eric was in Montana when the woman and her child were killed by someone she met online. And Eric was in the Florida Keys when the two guys were murdered and chopped up into little pieces."

Kadar interrupted Mark, "I think I know where you're going with this and I think you're way off base. I mean, I thought of it when Eric called me from Florida and when I realized the Montana murders happened when he was out there but he travels all around the country. He is on the road more than he is home. The odds of him being in a state when a murder occurs are pretty good. Murders happen all the time and Eric travels a lot."

Mark said, "I just found it suspicious that Eric was in both of those states on the exact dates the murders occurred. I'm not accusing him of anything, I'm just checking out a lead."

"I know Eric and he isn't capable of anything like that. But to prove it to you if you text me the dates and the location of the murders, I can check them against the texts Eric sent me. Out of boredom he texts me when he is on the road. You know just; How's it going? How's the book coming? I haven't deleted them. Don't ask me why, I never delete anything."

"Have you got a pencil and paper handy, I have the dates and locations right here, I can just read them to you," Mark said as he was searching through his document file for the information. "Okay, you ready?"

Mark read off the pertinent information, date and location for each of the murders that he thought might be similar to murders in the *Rampage* book; Bonnie Winslow being found in the Green River in Michigan, the Son of Sam look-alike murder of the two kids parked in a lover's lane in the Lake of the Ozarks area, the nurse in South Carolina who was suspected of killing her patients by injecting their IV bags with epinephrine, the pastor and his wife who were bludgeoned to death in Blackfoot,

Idaho, the murders of the co-eds in Madison and the murder and mutilation of the two men in Key West.

"Okay, I'll see what I can find out, but I'm telling you that this theory of yours won't hold water. But I will check it out just to put your mind at ease," Kadar said.

Mark said, "Like I said, I'm not accusing him of anything. I'm just checking everything out, leaving no stone unturned. You're probably right, he doesn't have anything to do with it but you know me and coincidences. Oh, and Skip, I would appreciate it if you don't mention this to Eric. He already doesn't like me and has threatened to kill me."

"Okay, I'll get back to you," the author said and hung up.

Mark stood up and walked to the kitchen for a beer, mumbling to himself, "What have I gotten myself into now. If Kadar and Eric are in this together, they now know I have figured it out and they might come after me. Shit, I just painted a great big target on my back."

He sat back down at the laptop and Sherry asked, "What's wrong, you look troubled. Is your stomach bothering you? Do you have gas?"

He looked at Sherry and said, "No, I don't have gas. If I did, don't you think you would have smelled it by now? I just have some questions bothering me about a murder I'm following." Mark didn't want to tell Sherry that he may have invited a murderer to come and kill him.

Chapter 40

Eric sat in a Cracker Barrel restaurant in Janesville, Wisconsin, eating a stack of pancakes, a double order of nearly raw bacon and three runny fried eggs. He brought his iPad in with him so he could check for some items he needed to kill Mark.

Since he would be making his way through Wisconsin visiting the Pump, Party and Play stores for the next week, he would order what he needed and have it delivered to general delivery in one of the northern Wisconsin towns. As he worked his way north checking stores, he'd pick it up at a town along the Wisconsin-Michigan border and, as he drove across the Upper Peninsula on the way back to his house in Lower Michigan, he would stop off and kill the man who was wrecking his plan; take him out of the equation. Then Kadar could announce the discovery of a copycat killer and receive the attention he deserved and sell a shit load of books.

It was winter in the Upper Peninsula which means snow, so Eric needed to buy some winter camouflage. He wanted to be white, from head to toe, white boots, white hat, white gloves and a white hood. He wanted to blend in when he snuck up to the cottage in hunt of his prey. He wanted the advantage. He wanted to see his victim but he didn't want his victim to see him. The element of surprise was crucial for his plan.

When he was in the Special Forces, Eric had a month of TWA; Tactical Winter Assault training. He was flown to the United States scientific research station aboard a LC-130 Hercules to the Amundsen–Scott South Pole Station.

Although the station was built for and professed the mission of scientific research, the military often used the facility for training troops for combat for northern climates in preparation for a possible invasion in areas of northern Europe. In addition to marksmanship and long range shooting, he was trained in a variety of techniques: detection, stalking, target range estimation, camouflage, infiltration, special reconnaissance and observation, surveillance and target acquisition. He was well trained for this mission. Taking out a civilian wouldn't be a problem.

As he passed through Marinette in northern Wisconsin, Eric located the post office and picked up his Amazon package from the general delivery window. The order was complete, no back orders, so he could proceed with his mission to eliminate his target. In a motel in Escanaba, Michigan, Eric tried on his winter camo. He looked in the bathroom mirror at his reflection and was pleased with what he saw. He was all white, from the hood covering his head to the white souled boots, there was even white mesh over the eye holes rendering the brown of his eye a milky white. He would be completely undetectable in the snow surrounding the reporter's cottage.

Eric's plan was to wait until three or four in the morning then silently make his way through the woods where his tracks in the snow would not be detected. Eric selected Friday to be the day Mark took his final breath. He checked the moon phase app on his phone, finding the moon would be in a waxing crescent so there would be very little lunar illumination. The weather app predicted a storm with heavy snow accumulation which would help to cover his car's tire tracks where he would turn off the highway onto the logging trail and it would cover his footprints through the forest.

Chapter 41

"It snowed again," Sherry said as she and the dog walked down from the loft.

Mark, who was sitting on the couch reading an article on the Detroit Free Press website looked up and said, "Yeah, what else is new. It's snowed every day for the last twenty seven days."

"But at least we have enjoyed watching Jake plowing and we have witnessed the formation of a new mountain. I mean, Mt. Jacob has grown right before our eyes," Sherry said as she shuffled by on the way to the bathroom.

Mark stood up and walked to the door to let the dog out and said, "You know, Mt. Jacob will probably still be there in July." He turned to the dog waiting by the door. "Come on you little ass sniffer, time to go out and tempt the eagle and fox." Mark watched the little dog tramp through the new layer of white stuff. The dog melted a little yellow hole in the snow with urine and ran back to the door, ready for the warmth of the cottage. Mark let her in and she shook the snow off. Mark was ready this time and he was wearing his slippers. As the dog ran off to sit outside the bathroom door, Mark turned off the lakeside flood lights, then walked to the north deck door to flip the lights off that illuminated that side and then to the back door to turn off the two flood lights that lit the garage and drive. He didn't normally leave the lights on all night but since Eric decided to make his threats, Mark felt better having the perimeter of the house bathed in light during the night.

During the winter months there were only three full time residences on the inland lake. Snow Plow Jake and his parents lived down the shore about half a mile and a retired electrician and his wife lived across the lake. All the other houses were summer cottages owned by people in town or from elsewhere in Michigan, Illinois or Wisconsin, so life at the Daniels cottage during the winter months was quite desolate. It was fourteen miles to the nearest town of Manistique, sixty miles to the shops in Escanaba and almost eighty miles to Marquette where the major chain stores were located. Mark and Sherry enjoyed the solitude most of the time but the winters seemed to be growing longer and less appealing. Next winter they would close the cottage for a month or so and go somewhere warm.

Sherry arrived from the bathroom in all her splendor, the loose fitting terry cloth robe which did nothing to display her charms, the old well-worn slippers, and hair that she tried to do something with but would not cooperate with her efforts without being washed first. Mark had her French vanilla concoction waiting at her chair when Sherry and the dog sat and reclined. "Did we get enough snow for Jake to plow?" Sherry asked.

"Not yet, but later today we're supposed to get dumped on, 8 to 10 inches the weather guessers are saying. You know we are going to owe Jake a bunch of money for plowing this year. Hell, I bet our bill alone will pay off his truck and buy him some new colored lights."

Sherry smiled and said, "Next year his truck will look like a Christmas tree."

Sherry finished her French vanilla about the same time she was done catching up on Facebook and said, "Do you want some breakfast? I feel like some eggs, and I think there are some sausage links in the freezer. How's an omelet sound?"

The snowy day was spent like most other winter days at the Daniels cottage. Mark scanned the computer for any murders that might be related to the *Rampage* book, shoveled the snow including twice shoveling the little fuzz bucket's path to the poop field. Sherry talked with Mickie, made lunch and cleaned the kitchen and bathroom. They talked about going to the Jack Pine for the whitefish special but decided to wait until later to decide. If the snowstorm was too bad they would eat something from the freezer. "Maybe meatballs, mashed potatoes, gravy and cream corn," Sherry thought, mentally preparing for the weather to cancel their date.

Coming in after the second shoveling, Sherry yelled from the loft bedroom where she was laying down after a hard day of doing very little, "Mark, your phone was ringing."

"Who was it?"

"I don't know; I was up here. I just lay down for a minute to cuddle with the princess but I guess I kind of fell asleep, and your cell woke me up."

Mark hung his coat and Stormy Kromer in the laundry room, kicked off his boots and walked to the kitchen for something to warm his innards. "I think a Manhattan would be good about now." He made one for himself and one for Sherry. He delivered the cocktail to Sherry who had arrived in her chair, then he went to check who had called him.

"It was Kadar," Mark said as he hit redial.

~ ~ ~

"Hey Skip, this is Mark," he said when the author answered on the second ring.

"Mark, thanks for getting back to me. Hey, I checked the locations and dates of the murders you found against the texts I received from Eric. We already knew Eric was in the Florida Keys when the guys were murdered and cut up and put in garbage bags. We figured out that he was in the vicinity of the woman who was killed in Montana around the same time she was killed and I found a text from Eric from Idaho around the time the pastor and his wife were murdered."

"So that puts him in the area during another murder; that's three. It's a little more than a coincidence," Mark said, quickly writing in his notebook.

"And Mark," Kadar said. "Eric was in Missouri when the kids were shot too. I know he was in Missouri but I don't know if he was in the Lake of the Ozarks area. Mark, do you think Eric could be going around killing people like the serial killers murdering people in my books?"

"I don't know Skip, but it certainly looks like it's a possibility. It may be just a huge coincidence but it's something we need to consider. Did you find any other dates and locations that corresponded with Eric's travels?"

"Well, I know that Eric was doing a Michigan run, visiting the Pump, Party and Play stores through the state when the girl found in the river was murdered," Kadar said.

"Bonnie Winslow?" Mark asked. "Was he in the northern lower peninsula?"

"I'm not sure. I know he was checking stores in rural Michigan but I'm not sure if he was in the Antrim County area. Probably, but I can't say for sure," the author said. "I'm not convinced Eric is involved with any of this; it might just be a coincidence. I mean, he travels all around the country and he is bound to be in a state when a murder happens. There are a lot of people in the state when a murder occurs and they are not involved in it," the author said.

Mark said, "I know, I didn't want to bring it up to you, but when you told me Eric was the one who told you about the two guys being murdered in the Keys and disposed of like Bob Berdella got rid of his victims in the *Rampage* book, and then that he told you about the woman and child murdered by a guy she met on line, just like the man who befriended women through the lonely hearts ads in newspapers in the book, I began to have suspicions. What we have uncovered is not an indictment of Eric, merely a strong suspicion. Maybe a coincidence but it's something we have to investigate. I know the evidence is damning, but it might just be circumstantial and turn out to be nothing." Mark hoped that by downplaying his suspicion that Eric was murdering people to generate interest in the *Rampage* book, he wouldn't piss off the author but it was something he had to pursue.

Mark asked, "Are there any other murders where Eric was in the state or region?"

"I don't think so," the author said, "but I'll keep checking. I may have missed something. Eric texts and emails me a lot. Oh crap, I haven't checked the emails. I'll check my email and get back to you".

Mark thought for a moment and asked, "Where is Eric now?"

"I don't really know. He usually doesn't tell me where he is going, he just texts or emails me once he is there and sitting around in a motel room."

"Skip, what does Eric text about?" Mark asked out of curiosity.

"Nothing really, just boring stuff about his job, traveling, promotion ideas for the book, and sometimes about women he meets on the road," Skip answered.

"Uh-huh," Mark said thinking, "What kind of promotion ideas?"

"Oh you know, setting up book signings at libraries and book stores, getting interviews on local talk radio and PBS TV stations."

"Did he say anything about murders where he was located at the time?" Mark asked.

"Well, of course he had a lot to say about the murders of the two guys in The Keys because he was getting the information from a motel employee at the same time it was being played out. He also wrote something I didn't think too much about at the time but now it seems a little unusual."

"What's that?" Mark asked.

"When he was in Missouri he sent me a text, something about too bad there's not a serial killer running around killing people. Just a minute let me see if I can find it, I wrote it down last night. Here it is."

"If there was an active serial killer murdering people it would create interest and the public would be more inclined to buy a book about serial killers."

"Now that I read it again it sounds pretty incriminating, doesn't it?" the author said.

Mark, trying to sound uncommitted said, "Well, it is definitely an unusual comment to make considering what we now know and the fact that he made it while he was in Missouri and the two kids were killed during the same time period."

Kadar promised to check his email for messages from Eric and he assured Mark he would call with the information. Mark pressed the end button and looked out the window wall. He could just barely make out the middle of the lake through the giant flakes that were falling. His mind wasn't on the weather, it was on Eric.

He thought about the conversation he just had with the author of *Rampage,* about Eric and the places he traveled and places people were dying in remarkably similar fashions as in the book. Mark picked up his pencil and notebook to re-read his scribbles then ripped them out to start a new page. At the top he wrote, "Eric's Travels," below, "Murders – Dates and States."

Mark did a web search for a Pump, Party and Play website. He found a map of the United States with little flags indicating all of their locations across the nation. He first looked to Florida and found seven stores in the Florida Keys. The first store was in Key Largo in the upper keys, then one each down US 1 in Tavernier, Islamorada, Marathon, Big Pine and two in Key West. Thinking to himself, "It's already been established by his own admission that Eric was in the Keys during the time the murders occurred. There are two stores in Key West, so it's safe to assume Eric was in Key West sometime during that time and the two men went missing from Key West. Kadar said Eric was staying at a motel in Key Largo so Eric had to travel up US 1 from Key West to Key Largo; the same route where the body parts were found in garbage bags. Also, Eric knew of the murders before they were made public. He says he heard it from a guy at the motel but how do I know that's true. I think I have to say this one is very suspicious."

Mark continued with his thoughts, "Kadar said that he received a text from Eric the same day the two kids were shot to death in the Lake of the Ozarks area. The poor innocent kids with the rest of their lives ahead of them and they were gunned down in an ambush as they were locked in a romantic embrace. Just like David Berkowitz who killed young couples in New York."

The Pump, Party and Play map revealed that there were stores in the larger cities of St. Louis, Jefferson City, Kansas City, and Springfield, but they also had stores in some of the more rural areas including one in Gravois Mills near where the two kids were found murdered.

Mark thought, as he was writing, "Eric had to have checked the Gravois Mills store, so that puts Eric in the same city where two victims had gone to see a movie and were murdered. It doesn't prove that Eric killed those kids but it looks very suspicious, especially when you add the fact that he was in the Keys when the two guys were murdered and their bodies mutilated and the woman and her child in Montana."

Mark next was going to look into the deaths of the pastor and his wife who were beaten to death with a sledgehammer. Mark moved the cursor on his laptop over the Pump, Party and Play map looking for stores in Idaho. There were two along I 86; one in Idaho Falls and one in American Falls. Mark traced the expressway with his finger and found, lying between the two cities on I 86, was the town of Blackfoot, Idaho. The reverend and his wife were murdered just north of Blackfoot, Idaho. "That puts Eric driving through Blackfoot on or near the date the murders occurred. Again, nothing to hang him for but when considering the Montana, Florida and Missouri murders there was a strong line of circumstantial evidence that pointed to Eric being a serial killer."

"So what are we doing about dinner? I'm getting hungry," Sherry asked, interrupting Mark's train of thought. Do you think we should brave the snow and venture out in the blizzard? Or do you trust me to cook?"

"I don't think we should go out. Let's spend a quiet, romantic evening here in our cozy little cabin. We'll dine on your delectable cuisine, sip from the nectar of the grape and make love by the light of the fireplace and to the sound of the howling wind and snow pelting the windows," Mark said, smiling at his wife.

"Are you sure? I may kill you with my cooking, you know. Do you really want your last breath to be smelling of meatballs and beef gravy?"

Chapter 42

Sherry's dinner was great, although when Mark developed heartburn he teased her that she had laced his meal with some of the rodent poison he set out in the basement and garage to deter the mice. A pill took care of the acid indigestion and they turned off all the downstairs lights except the exterior lights which Mark still left on, and they went up to the loft for some satisfying snow storm sex.

Sherry fell asleep right away and the dog was snoring but Mark lay awake, his mind consumed with the evidence that he and Kadar were compiling about Eric. It was sounding rather convincing that he was the serial killer roaming the country murdering innocent people to promote Kadar's new book.

Mark re-played the murders and Eric's connection; the guys in Florida being killed while Eric was there, the mother and child in Montana while Eric was in Montana, the kids shot to death in the Lake of the Ozarks while Eric was in Missouri. It all added up in Mark's mind as being beyond circumstantial. If only they could get ahold of Eric's travel records they could probably connect him to other murders in other states, but without a court order to release the travel documents, the Pump, Party and Play company I'm sure wouldn't make them available to a couple of writers if he and Kadar would ask.

~ ~ ~

As Eric drove from his motel room in Escanaba to the Daniels cottage on Dodge Lake, he mentally reviewed his mission. He had never been to the house but he knew intimately what the house looked like, both inside and out. He had hacked into Sherry's Facebook account, and during the remodeling of the cottage, Sherry had posted close to a hundred photographs. He knew where each entrance was, where the bedrooms were located, he was familiar with the loft where Mark and Sherry slept and he knew the layout of the building so well he was confident he could walk through the cottage in the dark.

An internet search of the Schoolcraft County records provided Eric with the description of the Daniels property; 9.5 acres, running 985 feet from Island Lake Road to the shore of Dodge Lake and approximately 200 feet along the lakeshore. From the county map that he had downloaded, he knew the lot was at one time a rectangle, but two lots on the lake had been sold off.

Eric zoomed in on the Google Earth app to get a view of the terrain of the Daniels property. The house and garage took up most of the cleared portion of the property. About four acres was covered in new growth hardwood and the remainder of the property was covered in pine trees planted in long straight rows decades before Mark and Sherry purchased the property. On the Google Earth image, Eric located what looked like an old logging trail about two miles from the Daniels property where he could park his car out of view of vehicles on the highway. There weren't any homes or cabins down the trail so no one should be driving on it to notice a car parked in a place where a car shouldn't be parked. He developed his strategy using all the intel available to him.

~ ~ ~

Eric turned off US 2 onto north M 94 towards the Daniels cottage. He drove about 14 miles north, located the logging trail and parked his car. He used the serrated portion of his knife to cut a low-lying branch from a pine tree. Between the heavy snow, which was beginning to drift as the wind picked up, and the pine branch, Eric obscured his tire tracks off the highway onto the old logging trail.

Content his tire tracks would not be noticed, especially with the heavy snow falling, he began to walk through the woods dragging the pine branch behind him to obscure his footprints. So far his plan was working to perfection.

He arrived near the Daniels cottage in less than a half hour. Eric could have remained there in the woods about 100 yards from the house and waited until his target came out of the house then with one squeeze of his trigger finger, a .338 magnum slug from a scoped Remington M24 sniper rifle, traveling at 2,580 feet per second would enter his brain, scramble his gray matter then exit out the back of his head sending shards of skull, brain and blood for twenty feet. But that wasn't how he wanted to kill the reporter. Shooting him from 300 feet was too impersonal; Eric wanted Mark to know who was killing him. He didn't even bring a firearm, just a knife. He wanted Mark to look into his eyes as he slit his throat. He wanted to see Mark's face the moment he realized he was going to die. Eric wanted to watch the blood drain from Mark's body.

Eric stood motionless in the woods mentally preparing himself. He had planned this mission right down to the smallest detail but he had not planned on finding the house brightly illuminated in the middle of the night. Every exterior light of the cottage was lit and the house, garage and the drive area were bathed in light. "Just a minor problem," Eric thought. He would need to eliminate the lights for his plan to succeed.

From his vantage point in the woods, he studied the house through a small pair of night vision goggles. In his Special Forces training he was taught various methods to render a dwelling in the dark. The first and by far quickest was to use a pair of insulated cable cutters and cut the electrical feed leading into the electrical box usually mounted on the exterior of a building. Since he didn't have cable cutters he moved on to option two. The electrical box was mounted at the rear of the house. "I can make my way to the box, break the wire tag securing the box closed, open the box and remove the meter. No electricity entering the house equals no lights shining outside." However, to get to the electrical box he would need to walk through the yard, being exposed and leaving obvious footprints. If anyone were to get up to pee and looked out at the snow they would surely see the footprints and be alerted to his presence. He'd have to go to the next location the electricity could be shut off, the breaker box, probably in the basement.

He studied the house. "If I walk through the woods to a point further down the driveway and cross it there, my foot prints would not be visible from the house. Then I can walk through the woods on that side of the drive almost to the north side of the structure to the walkout basement door," Eric thought. "The lock on the door is probably a cheap door knob lock that I can easily open."

~ ~ ~

Mark lay in bed staring at the ceiling thinking about Eric and the murders until a hog grunted and its coarse whiskers brushed against his belly as the beast took a bite. "No, not again, no!" Mark yelled in his dream. The vile odor of rotten table scraps mixed with the stench of pig shit crept from Mark's subconscious. He was lying in the mud and pig manure while the vision of pigs chewing parts of his body filled his brain. A large sow was gnawing on one of his arms, three fingers already missing from the hand. He looked down the length of his body, both his feet were gone, a large gaping, bloody hole was where his stomach should have been and his penis was missing. "No, not my dick! No, no, no! God help me!"

~ ~ ~

Eric cautiously walked to the basement door, finding the lock wasn't much of a deterrent to someone with his skills and he was soon in the dark basement. Through the night vision goggles, Eric located the breaker box hung on the cement block wall of the basement. He walked to it and slowly and silently opened the panel door. His white-gloved fingers gripped the main breaker at the top of the box and pulled it down. The breaker halted the flow of electricity entering the house with a loud thud. "Shit!" Eric silently said. The sound was louder than he anticipated. "Hopefully the people sleeping two flights up in the loft didn't hear it."

~ ~ ~

A hog was waddling across the pen towards him and Mark tried to kick it away but there was no leg from his knee down, he was just waving around a thigh that ended in a bloody stump. "I'm just inviting the beast to feast on the meat of my thigh." Mark's vision was blurred with blood running down his face from where the swine had gnawed on the side of his head, "No, please don't, I can't take it anymore!"

As the hog took a bite of Marks thigh he heard the dog barking. "Yes, go get help!" he yelled to the dog, "Go get mom, she'll know what to do, she can call 911. And get an ambulance and the police or maybe animal control. Hurry and get her. Quit barking and go get mom, you mangy bag of fleas! Go get mom!"

"Why won't the dog quit barking? The little shit won't scare the pigs away, hell the mutt will probably end up being their dessert. I bet the little hair ball is barking in joy. It's probably happy I'm being consumed by the pigs. I won't be around so it won't have to share Sherry's attention anymore. You'll have her all to yourself. You jealous little piss bucket. Go get mom!"

Suddenly Mark noticed the foul odor was gone and that he wasn't in the pigpen any longer. The pigs had disappeared. He looked and he had all of his appendages, a quick check revealed his penis was intact. "A nightmare, just another fucking nightmare!" Mark said noticing he hadn't awakened Sherry.

As he lay in bed, his pulse racing and the sheets drenched with sweat, Mark realized the dog really was barking. The little princess was downstairs barking at something. Mark grabbed the flashlight from the bedside stand and went downstairs to find the dog standing by the door to the basement. She was looking at the door and barking her irritating yappy bark. "Shut up you little asshole!" Mark said in a hushed tone. He opened the door and flipped the light switch but no light came on. "Oh, great and now we've lost power, damn storm!" With flashlight lit, Mark descended into the darkness of the basement looking for assassins, butchers, murderers, and pigs.

The dog barked and Mark looked back at the little old Yorkie standing at the top of the stairs. "What's wrong with you, not so brave are we?" You'll stand at the top of the stairs and make a bunch of noise but you're too chicken to come downstairs with me. You K9 coward!"

~ ~ ~

At the first bark, Eric quickly moved behind a partial wall that hid the water pump and hot water heater. He didn't want to be discovered by Mark. The hallmark of his plan was the element of surprise. He didn't want to be found by his prey; he wanted to do the finding.

Eric silently stood motionless, ready to pounce on the reporter if he had to and kill him on the spot but he preferred to take him out later in the daylight so he could watch Mark die. And if that fucking yappy mutt came downstairs, it would surely sniff him out but Eric planned a contingent for that too; his big hand would squeeze the little dog's throat until all the bark and breath had left its body.

Mark shined the flashlight around. Nothing seemed out of place. If he had a reason to shine the light towards the floor he would have noticed wet footprints leading from the door to the electrical panel and behind the partition. But Mark didn't and seeing nothing out of the ordinary, he swore at the dog and climbed the basement stairs. The dog at the top of the stairs looked down at him and barked a few more times before Mark made a lunging move towards the little beast and yelled, "Shut up, you rat faced yappy creature!" The dog ran on her little seven-inch Yorkie legs through the living room, up the stairs and jumped in bed with Sherry.

As Mark crawled into bed Sherry sleepily asked, "What's wrong with the princess? Did she need to go pee pee?"

"No, your yappy little dog just likes to wake me up and make me run around the house in my underwear. Oh, and the storm knocked the power out."

~ ~ ~

Eric, as stealthily as possible, walked to the basement door and exited, closing the door with only a barely audible click of the latch making contact with the striker plate, a sound heard only by the dog lying in bed in the loft. She barked at the noise but when Mark kicked at her she jumped out of the way and crawled up to the safety of Sherry's arms. Mark laughed to himself, at least he was able to kick out with more than just a bloody stump, with more than a pig appetizer.

Eric carefully walked back into the woods and crossed the driveway making sure to step in his previous tracks and returned to the wooded area at the back of the house.

Eric stood secluded in the woods near the driveway and surveilled the area. He noticed the snow shovel leaning against the garage. "He'll need that in the morning," Eric surmised. "When he goes for the shovel I'll take him out."

Eric was trained to keep the advantage on his side and the advantage he had over his prey in this situation was surprise. He would stay hidden until his victim was within striking range then with arms raised to increase his physical presence and screaming to scare his prey into a paralyzing state of shock, he would pounce on the reporter, immediately grab him from behind and place the sharpened edge of his knife against the man's throat just below the ear. Eric closed his eyes to visualize the knife cutting into the flesh, severing the carotid artery, increasing pressure as he dragged the blade across the cartilage of the trachea and continued to the jugular.

As Mark's heart pumped its last beats, the blood would spurt from the severed artery and vein. Eric expected to be bloodied and had a plan already in place to deal with the soiled white camo. He had a burlap bag in his car. He would stuff the bloody camo in it and on the way back to his motel in Escanaba he would toss it into the Rapid River, which he had noticed was not entirely frozen over, and flowing quickly towards Lake Michigan. The rocks Eric put in the bag would carry the bag and its bloody contents to the bottom of the river and the current would take it out into the lake. It might be eventually found but it would be long after Eric had left the area and could not possibly be tracked back to him. To protect his identity when purchasing the camo, Eric used a post office general delivery as an address, a fictitious name, a phony email account and a credit card he took out under a false name.

Looking back at the snow shovel next to the garage, Eric thought of things that could go wrong so he would be prepared to handle them if the need should arise. There were two adults and a little fucking ankle biter in the house. His target was the reporter but if his wife came outside with Mark, Eric would first take out Mark and then his wife. She would be easy; she would be in a mental stupor after watching her husband's throat being slit from ear to ear. As she stood in horror looking at the snow turned red with her husband's blood, Eric would quickly grab her and slit her throat too.

He needed to determine where to wait in hiding for his target to make an appearance. For his plan to work to its utmost effectiveness, Eric needed to remain unseen by his victim as he walked towards the garage to get the snow shovel, yet he had to be close enough to his target to quickly close the distance between them before the reporter had time to make sense of the situation and react. Eric thought, "The old fight or flight response would be triggered if Eric didn't get to his victim and take him out quickly. If the reporter tried to run, Eric was sure he could catch him and if he tried to fight, Eric had no doubt he would easily overpower the man. In either scenario Eric would be able to complete his mission but both were sloppy and Eric was anything but sloppy. He took pride in being methodical, precise and tactically correct.

If he were to remain in the woods just off the driveway, he would need to cover a distance of approximately thirty to thirty three feet. His target would see and hear him coming; he would lose the element of surprise so he had to be as close to Mark as possible. He looked at the snow pile next to the driveway and thought about crouching behind it. He would be concealed and closer to his prey but he would not be able to see his victim as he exited the house and walked to the garage. He next considered hiding on the side of the garage away from the house; it offered cover from the house, and a close proximity to where the reporter would be when he grabbed the snow shovel but again he wouldn't be able to see Mark until the last minute.

Eric looked around from his location in the woods and noticed a place where he would be hidden yet be just a few feet from the snow shovel and his target. It was a location his instructors at the TWA Training would consider tactically spot-on. It would require Eric to call on his training in winter camouflage and his ability to remain perfectly still for a long period of time. He could lie in front of the snow pile at the side of the driveway. The snow was falling so heavy and the wind blowing it into drifts that his shape would quickly be obscured making him invisible to his unsuspecting target. He would just be another non-descript lump in the snow, just a snowdrift in the driveway.

He would need to remain motionless, not a problem for Eric. He could lay and wait for hours to accomplish his mission if he needed to. He was an extremely patient person. The vantage point provided him an unobstructed view of the back door of the cottage; he could watch Mark when he left the cottage, as he stepped down off the porch and walked to the garage to get the snow shovel. Eric liked the location, he would be just feet from his prey and could easily jump up from a prone position and within a few steps be slicing the man's throat. "Yes, this location works best," Eric thought as he lowered himself down in the fresh snow in front of the snow pile. He lay on his left side holding the knife at the ready in his right hand.

He laid motionless as the snow fell and accumulated on him. Eric's head was covered with a white hood with white mesh for eyeholes and over his body he wore a white insulated jump suit. Eric held the knife within his white-gloved hand and his boots were white leather with white rubber soles all combining to make him blend in with his surroundings. The falling and drifting snow would accumulate on him and further obliterate his shape, rendering him nearly invisible. It was all coming together. Now he just had to be patient and wait.

~ ~ ~

Mark, as usual, awoke at 5:17 according to his cell phone. The electricity was still off so that meant no light, no computer and no coffee. Mark looked out the lakeside windows and, despite not having any exterior lights, he guessed they had gotten about ten to twelve inches of snow overnight, maybe more since it was hard to tell with the drifting. He figured once the sun rose in the east, he would go out and shovel the back porch, a path to the garage, the front deck and the poop field.

Mark was sitting in a recliner with the gas fireplace casting its warm glow around the room reading USA Today and using up data on his cell phone when Sherry and the dog came down. It was early for the two of them to be climbing out of bed; it wasn't quite 7:10.

"Good morning, sweetheart," Sherry said as she descended the stairs from the loft. She paused to kiss Mark on the top of his head.

Mark said, "I hope I didn't wake you up last night with my nightmare. But I bet your dog probably woke you if I didn't."

"No, I didn't hear a thing. You know what too much wine can do to me. I was out all night. How about you hon, are you all right? Was it a bad nightmare?" she asked as she walked towards the bathroom.

"It was okay, but this time your yappy dog was in the dream." Sherry closed the bathroom door as Mark yelled, "Hey, Sher, the power is out so don't flush the toilet. There's no electricity so the pump isn't pumping and the toilet won't refill, and I don't want to be melting buckets of snow just to flush a toilet. Remember that old saying, "If it's brown flush it down, if it's yellow let it mellow."

A voice from inside the bathroom told Mark, "Well, you better melt some snow because this one is being flushed."

"What's wrong with you, you yappy little bag of dog farts?" Mark asked the dog who was sitting at the lakeside door barking at him. "Need out? You're not going to like it." Mark looked out the window and saw a two-foot drift at the door. "Come on piss head you're going out back."

The dog reluctantly followed Mark to the rear door and stepped out into snow almost deeper than it was tall. The little Yorkie pushed its way through the snow to the edge of the porch, looked towards Mt. Jacob and started barking.

Mark opened the screen door, looked around the yard and asked, "Now what's wrong with you?" The dog looked back at Mark then turned back towards the snow pile and barked. "Come on in, you little shit, you'll wake the dead."

The dog squatted and peed then turned towards the door, stopped on the floor mat to shake the snow from her body and ran in to take up its sentry post at the bathroom door awaiting the appearance of its human. Mark looked around the yard again thinking there must be a raccoon or maybe a deer nearby that got the dog riled up. "I hope it's not a fox this close to the house."

"Did princess go out and go pee pee and poop poop?" Sherry asked as she emerged from the bathroom, the toilet making a recently flushed gurgling sound.

"No, she peed but the snow is way too deep for her to squat and crap. I'll have to go out and shovel for her. But, first I'm going to figure out a way to make a pot of coffee."

Sherry looked at her husband and asked, "And how are you going to do that? The stove is electric and even the hot water heater is electric so there's no hot water."

"Just watch me. Where there is a will there is a way."

Sherry responded, "No, where there is an addiction there is an addict who will do whatever necessary to sedate his cravings."

"You call it an addiction; I call it an appreciation for the coffee beans that grow in the mountainous region of Columbia." Mark kicked off his slippers, put on his boots and a coat. He went to the kitchen for a pot and walked out the north door to the snow covered deck. With gloved hands he brushed the snow from the gas grill and pulled off the frozen and stiff plastic cover. With a little difficulty he was able to get a flame and put the pot filled with snow over it. He kept adding snow as it melted until he had a full pot of hot water. As he opened the door, careful not to spill his treasure, Sherry took the pot and handed him an empty pot. "Thanks, I need this to wash up. Here, use this for coffee water."

Mark just rolled his eyes at Sherry. He knew it would be useless to argue. "Hey, get me the mop bucket; I might as well get some snow melted to flush the toilet."

~ ~ ~

Eric lay under several inches of snow that had drifted over his form; he was completely concealed. "The reporter didn't see me even though he was looking right at me, but that fucking dog has to go. I have studied people and their intricacies but animals are way too unpredictable. That dog knew I was here. It was barking at me but Mark wasn't smart enough to listen to the animal."

All the while the dog was barking at the snow pile and Mark was at the door, Eric was thinking what he would do if the dog were to run to the unusual snow drift with a human scent and start to dig. "I would need to react quickly, forget about the dog and jump up and run towards the house. If I'm fast enough and Mark is sufficiently traumatized by my appearance I can get to him before he thinks of closing and locking the door."

Luckily the dog went back in and Mark followed. "I need to be patient," Eric told himself. "He will be out to shovel soon. The snow was so deep the dog wouldn't leave the porch. Mark knows he has to get out and shovel. It will just be a matter of time."

Within minutes the back door opened and Mark, wearing a winter coat and red and black plaid wool hat, came out on the porch. Eric was ready, his body was like a wound spring ready to pounce the second the opportunity presented itself.

The dog and Mark walked out on the porch and realized the snow shovel wasn't there. He forgot that he had left it leaning against the garage yesterday when he finished shoveling for the second time. Mark took a step off the porch into the deep snow and began to walk towards the garage to get the shovel.

Eric's muscles tensed. He was ready. This is what he was waiting all night for, why he stayed awake preparing for the kill. All of his hard work and careful planning was about to come to fruition. Soon he would slit the throat of his nemesis and hold his body while it took its dying breath and watch as his heart pumped the last of his blood on the snow. His mission would be accomplished.

Mark stopped after only two steps when the dog started barking frantically "What's up now dipshit?" The dog stood on the porch looking at Mark and barking its high shrill bark. Mark returned to the porch and opened the screen door to let the dog in. With a pissed look, Mark began to swipe his foot back and forth pushing the snow off the porch, making a small clearing for the dog.

Mark would never know that the terrible terrier, yapping Yorkie, mange mutt, piss bucket, shit machine, flea bag, fuzz nut, dipshit dog, hairball, eagle bait, ass sniffing and butt licking little dog... had just saved his life.

Eric watched the reporter stomp his feet, trying to get the snow from his boots and pants legs before he walked back inside. Five minutes later the door opened and the little barking mutt came out. It sniffed the air, looked at the snow pile and started barking again. The dog stopped barking long enough to squat and leave a little pile of steaming crap on the porch. The door opened and Mark called the dog back inside. Eric noticed Mark no longer had his coat and hat on. He would need to be patient a little longer.

The dog's barking didn't give away his presence and with a snowdrift covering his head Eric was pretty well insulated from the high pitched barking of the dog. He could hardly hear it.

Mark appeared at the door again. He opened the screen door and had to place his foot in the opening to prevent the barking dog from running out. "What's wrong with you? Most of the time I can't get you to go out, and now you won't stay in?" Mark looked out down the driveway, listened for a moment, turned, went back inside and closed the door.

Mark walked into the living room to stand in front of the fireplace to chase the chill from his body. Even with dry socks replacing those that got wet when he cleaned the porch with his foot, he was having trouble warming up. Sherry brought him a cup of hot coffee and said, "Thanks for taking care of the princess. I'm sure she appreciates it." She lifted the dog up to Mark and said, "Tell daddy thank you." Sherry pushed the animal towards him and made its paw shake up and down and mouthed, "Thank you daddy. You're such a good daddy."

Mark gave a slight smile, sipped his coffee hoping Sherry would move the dog out of his face before he would need to respond to the spoiled little mutt. She didn't, so he had to reply to the animal that smelled like wet dog, "You're welcome princess."

"Mark I forgot to tell you that I got a text from Jake that he was going in to work a couple of hours late today because of the snow and would be down in a while to plow us out. And when I asked if he heard anything about how long the electricity would be out and he said they have power at his house. It must be a line down out our way."

Mark said, "I thought I could hear Jake plowing. He should be up at the house in a few minutes."

~ ~ ~

Eric lay motionless as the dark green F150 slowly crept towards the garage, lowered his blade and backed off, pulling the snow away from the garage door. He carefully crept forward again to pull another eight-foot wide swath away from the garage door. Mark usually shoveled the snow from in front of the garage door so Jake wouldn't have to do the precision plowing close to the door. He didn't do it so much to help out Jake but to keep the eight foot long piece of curved steel attached to a powerful 5.4 liter engine controlled by a reckless kid away from the garage door. But there was just too much snow for Mark to mess with this morning.

Eric lay still, only moving his eyes following the movement of the pick-up truck. This was something he had not anticipated but it was nothing he couldn't handle. If the plow got too close to him he would just have to kill the driver, simple collateral damage.

The truck backed out of his path of vision. He could hear the truck continue to back up. "He's leaving. Backing out of the path he plowed," Eric thought, wishing he could turn his head and see where the truck was without giving his position away. "He probably just did a quick job and will come back to widen out the drive when he finishes the rest of his customers. I've seen it done that way before, just open up a lane for the people to get out then come back later and clean it up."

"Mark!" Sherry yelled from the back door. "Are you ready for the show? Come on honey or you'll miss it. He's backing up towards the edge of the woods and is almost ready to plow the snow into Mt. Jacob."

"Just a minute, I'm peeing." Mark was zipping up as he ran to the back door, arriving just in time to see Jake put the truck into first gear, rev the engine sending a cloud of black smoke out the dual exhaust pipes. The nineteen year old, with a look of crazed amusement on his face, popped the clutch and all four of the oversized heavily treaded tires showing a trace of green LED lights reflecting off the chrome wheels bit into the snow and the truck lurched forward pushing a huge mound of snow before it. The small unusually shaped pile in front of the mountain was no deterrent for the truck moving at nearly 20 miles per hour when it smashed into the snow mountain. Jake continued backing and racing forward pushing snow deeper on the mountain, compressing the loose packed snow into a tightly packed mass.

"That is fun to watch," Mark admitted to Sherry. "Do you think we should tip Jake for entertaining us during these boring winter months?"

"Probably, how big do you think that mountain will get? There is still a lot of winter left and a lot more snow to pile up," Sherry asked.

"The mountain may not get much higher but the pile will get wider as he keeps pushing the snow up against it. I bet we will still have snow there in June. Come on, Sher, let's make a bet. I say the last snow of Mt. Jacob won't melt until June 15th. What's your date?"

"Hmmm, I bet it won't be totally melted until at least June 20th. What are we betting? A buck, do you want to make it five, big spender?"

Mark smirked at his wife and said, "I was thinking something a little more of a sexual nature, myself." A backhand to his gut as she walked away was Sherry's response to his proposal. "Okay, five bucks; lets write the dates on the calendar before we forget them."

~ ~ ~

Eric never saw the big curved blade of the snowplow as it raced forward and slammed into him and smashed his crumbled body into the densely packed snow of Mt. Jacob. He lay buried in the hard packed snow alive but unable to move. "Is the snow so tightly packed that I can't move or..." A sickening thought crossed his mind, "am I paralyzed?" he asked himself. "I don't feel any pain, I could be paralyzed. I have to stop the truck before it plows into the pile again. Stop!" he yelled, but the word didn't come out of his mouth.

The realization that he could do nothing was a shock to Eric. Being completely powerless was a strange sensation to him. He was always in control of the circumstances and of himself. He was always the determining factor in any situation, yet now all he could do was lay there and listen. Listen to the sound of the truck backing off, listen to the sound of the pneumatic cylinders lower the heavy steel blade of the plow to the ground, listen to the truck revving its engine then listen to the truck powering forward, pushing another load of snow into the tightly packed mass of Mt. Jacob. Eric listened no more.

Chapter 43

"For the last couple of weeks, your little designer dog wants to go out back to pee and poop instead of where I shoveled down to the frozen grass out front. What's with that? She never wanted to go out back before."

"I know, and she keeps barking at Mt. Jacob too," Sherry added.

Mark opened the door and bristled at the temperature. "It's gotta be five to ten below zero out there and that's without figuring in the wind. With the wind chill I bet its 20 to 30 degrees below zero," he yelled to Sherry who was sitting next to the fire sipping her creamer and coffee. "At these temperatures Mt. Jacob might become a glacier and last a lot longer than either of us planned. Heck, I bet professors from the university up in Marquette will come to explore and dig for mastodons and other life forms frozen in the ice, maybe a cave man like they found in Europe or Russia or Antarctica, anyway they found one somewhere." Mark opened the door and yelled, "Come on in you Yappy Yorkie." The dog was busy sniffing and barking at the six-foot high pile of snow.

"Oh, you are so full of crap," Sherry said looking up from the tablet where she was checking Facebook. "And before you ask, No, you cannot change your date for the great Mt. Jacob Melting Challenge."

Mark lifted his empty coffee cup to Sherry in a non-verbal way of asking if she wanted a refill. She silently held her cup up indicating hers was still full and he walked to the kitchen.

~ ~ ~

Sherry yelled to her husband from her chair, "Did you ever hear back from the electric company about the fuse blowing during that storm?"

"Yeah, they said there was probably a surge in the power and it tripped the breaker. By the way, we don't have fuses we have circuit breakers. They said it doesn't happen very often but sometimes it does."

"You mean we sat in the dark for three days, melting snow for washing, cooking and flushing until you went downstairs to check the stupid thing," Sherry said enjoying getting the best of Mark for a change. "What's the matter with you? Are you afraid of the basement, afraid the boogieman down there is gonna get you?" she teased, trying to make a spooky boogieman face.

Mark had to admit that it was pretty silly that he didn't even think about the breaker until the lady at the electric company asked if he had checked it. He did, then had to apologize to the lady who he was giving grief because they had not been out to restore their service. Before she hung up, the woman sarcastically explained that there were stores without power with their frozen food inventory melting, and a senior citizen home with freezing seniors, which was more important than him not being able to surf the Internet.

"How about the nightmares?" Sherry asked as Mark settled onto the couch. "I've been reluctant to bring them up but seems like you haven't had one in a couple of weeks."

"Yeah, it's been awhile. It feels good to be able to sleep through the night without waking up in a cold sweat with a pounding heart. And I haven't been getting up at 5:17 either. It's still early but 6:23 is a whole lot better than 5:17 am. I wonder what I'd find if I looked up every 23rd verse of the sixth chapter in every book of the Bible."

Sherry went to the bookshelf next to the fireplace, removed the Bible, handed it to Mark and said, "Here you might as well get looking before it drives you crazy." Mark discovered Romans 6:23: "For the wages of sin is death."

Sherry refilled their coffee cups and returned her attention to a recipe for scalloped potatoes someone had posted on Facebook.

"I'm going to give Kadar a call and see if he's heard anything about Eric," Mark said to Sherry. "It's been a week since I've heard from him; I wonder if there's anything new."

The author picked up on the first ring, "Hello?"

"Hey Skip, it's Mark, I'm just checking in to see if there is any news about Eric."

"No, nothing. This is very unusual for him. He always called, emailed or texted at least once a week. It's like he just vanished off the face of the earth. He hasn't called anyone or shown up for work. They even called me to see if I knew anything. I guess they found my number in his work address book."

"Did they say anything?" Mark asked.

"Yeah, they told me Eric was using his company credit card for meals, gas and lodging while he was checking stores throughout Wisconsin and the last charge was for a motel room in Escanaba. They said they told the police but they didn't find anything out of the ordinary."

"Who called the police?" Mark asked.

"Eric's daughter hadn't heard from him and he wasn't answering his cell so she checked with Pump, Party and Play and they told her that he hadn't been into work either."

Mark asked, "He has a daughter?"

"Yeah, Virginia. She must be 22 or 23 by now. Eric raised her since her mother was killed in a skiing accident when Ginny was just a child. She's a cardiology rehabilitation nurse at Henry Ford Hospital. That's down in Detroit."

"Yes, I'm familiar with where the hospital is," Mark said.

"Oh, yeah, I forgot that you used to live down here. Anyway, Ginny called the police and filed a missing person report."

Kadar continued, "The police checked Eric's phone record and it hasn't sent or received a call in a couple of weeks and a check of his personal credit cards showed they haven't been used either."

"What about his car?"

"Nothing. His car hasn't been seen since he checked into the motel. The police have a notice out for it but nothing has turned up so far. It's like he just disappeared."

"Maybe he was abducted? Or maybe he was in an accident and drove off the road and is in a ditch or down a cliff and the accident hasn't been discovered yet," Mark said coming up with plausible explanations as to how Eric might have vanished. "It's snowed so much up here lately his car could be covered and no one would see it till the spring melt."

The author finally broached the subject they both were hesitant to bring up, "Mark, do you think maybe Eric figured out we were investigating his possible involvement in the murders? Maybe he took off because we were getting too close to the truth."

Mark said, "Yeah, that could very well be a reason for him to take off, but did he know we made a connection and were checking him out? I didn't let him know. In fact I haven't talked to him since he threatened to kill me. Have you told him anything?"

"No, not a word," Kadar said. "We texted while he was in Wisconsin but it was about a book signing he was setting up with some Mystery Readers group in Saginaw.

He gave me the date, location and time and checked to make sure I had plenty of books to take to sell, but nothing to lead me to believe he knew we were checking out his possible involvement in murder."

"You know Skip, we need to tell the police what we discovered about the murders and the fact that Eric was in or near some of the locations when the murders were committed. They need to know that and it might have something to do with his disappearance."

"Yeah, I know. But I don't think Eric would just take off. He has Ginny. He wouldn't just leave without saying anything to her. No, I think something terrible happened to him."

Chapter 44

"I packed some clothes in the suitcase for you but you should really check them. I don't want to hear you complain that I packed the wrong stuff," Sherry yelled down from the loft.

"Okay, I'll check it out, but not right now. Heck, Sher, we don't leave for another two days," Mark said as he was collating and stapling piles of paper. He knew Sherry was excited about going to Mickie's house for Christmas. He was anxious to see her too, and they would be staying at her house. Her husband relented on the dog situation. Mark had gathered all he had on Eric being involved in the murders around the country and made photocopies; he and Kadar made an appointment with Detective Alfred Davis of the Northville Police Department. Eric lived in Northville so that's where Ginny filed the missing person report.

~ ~ ~

As they left the police station, Mark turned to Kadar and said, "That's done. Well, probably not done but we did our duty and turned over everything we had to them and now they can figure it out."

Kadar stopped and asked, "But, the detective didn't have to get all pissed off and yell at us for not telling them until now.

"Well, I can see his point. We should have told the police as soon as we suspected something. Technically, we were withholding important evidence about several unsolved murders. I know we didn't have a lot of information but I think we both knew that Eric might be involved somehow."

"Yeah, but he called us a couple of amateur sleuths, getting in the way of the professionals who do real police work. How did he put it? We were meddling in places where we shouldn't have been meddling. That was uncalled for. And I gave him a copy of *Rampage* and even autographed it too."

Mark said, "We have not heard the last from the detective. I'm sure he will be calling for more information and then, since the murders took place in multiple states, the case will probably be turned over to the FBI and they will be paying us a visit. This might drag on for several months or longer if they don't find Eric." Mark decided to change the subject, "Hey, want to get a cup of coffee?"

Over coffee and donuts at a Tim Horton's, Kadar asked Mark, "How's your book coming?" Kadar knew Mark was writing a novel based on a serial killer stalking people around the Lake of the Ozarks and in other locations throughout the Midwest.

"Good at times, and not so good at other times. Some days I can sit and write for hours and other days I just stare at the computer for hours," Mark answered. "How about yours?"

Kadar had earlier asked if Mark minded if he wrote the story of Eric. "I am concentrating on the background information right now and I'm sure I will be getting plenty of information now from the police, and like you said, if the FBI gets involved from them too. But, I am missing one major part to the book."

Mark wiped his mouth with a napkin after finishing his cream filled donut and asked, "What's that?"

Kadar looked up from studying his coffee and said, "A conclusion."

The men parted and promised to stay in touch and share anything they heard from the police. They had become friends; friends who shared the love of writing, who shared the intrigue of a good murder and shared a connection through Eric, although Eric was a friend of Kadar's and he wanted to kill Mark.

~ ~ ~

Mark and Sherry arrived back at the cottage after dark and after battling periodic whiteout conditions blowing off Lake Michigan and almost driving off the road into the ditch when an oncoming car started sliding sideways on the icy roads. All they wanted to do was go inside their cozy cottage, start the fire, pour a drink and relax. The trip north had stressed both of them.

The next morning Mark woke up at 6:23, pulled on his old terry cloth robe, went downstairs, flicked the switch to light the fireplace, started the coffee maker, went pee and turned on the laptop. He perused the news until he heard the dog jump off the bed. Mark stood by the lakeside door to let her out but the dog ran to the back door. She sat by the door and defiantly barked at Mark until he walked to the back door to let her out. "You still want to do your job out back, huh? Okay you maligned K9, go out and pee, but watch out for the eagle. It'll swoop down and grab you in its talons and carry you off to its nest and all we will find is your pretty pink collar and dog tags."

The dog ran out the door, stopped on the porch and stood barking at the snow pile across the driveway. Mark looked out and noticed Mt. Jacob had a hole in it. Something had been digging and a lot of the pile was strewn over the driveway. "What the hell?" Mark said, watching the little dog sniff around the pile. I didn't notice that last night, but then all I wanted to do when we got here was get out of the car."

"Come on you crapping creature," Mark called to the dog, "Come on in. I have to make your Mom's creamer and coffee." The dog sniffed and ran back to the porch and hopped inside.

It didn't take long for Sherry and Mark to fall into their usual routine. Mark thought, "I guess that's what retired people do. They get comfortable doing the same thing each day and it becomes a routine." They had eaten lunch and now he was sitting on the couch working on the computer and Sherry sat in her recliner checking Facebook and scratching the dog. She asked Mark, "What are we doing tonight? It's New Year's eve you know."

Mark was so engrossed with writing he had almost forgotten about the holiday. "I thought we could go out to Jack Pine. They have some dinner specials tonight. The all you can eat perch plate sounds good to me, and I think they are serving the roast beef you liked last time you had it," Mark said. "Want to go? I'll call and see if we need reservations."

Sherry told the dog to jump down and stood up. "Well, why didn't you tell me we had plans for New Years. I have to pick something out to wear and shower and do my hair and make up my face."

Mark looked at her and said, "It's the Jack Pine Lodge on M 94, not Sardi's on Times Square."

Sherry looked at him and said, "I don't care, its New Year's Eve!"

~ ~ ~

The parking lot at the Jack Pine was overflowing. There were pickup trucks with plows hanging off their front, SUV's of all makes and vintage, several Jeep Wranglers from an off roaders club, a bunch of four wheelers and a lot of snow machines parked on the snow covered horseshoe courts. When Sherry and Mark arrived they ordered drinks and stood waiting for a table and talking to the couple who lived across the lake. Mark was making up a story about a fox, trying to explain why their lights were on all night.

He looked around the bar and Mark noticed the women were dressed in anything from jeans and a sweatshirt to slacks and sweaters. Mark thought Sherry was over dressed but she explained she was dressed in a backwoods chic style.

Jake walked by and Mark yelled to him.

"Hey Mr. and Mrs. Daniels, how ya doin'? Happy New Year."

"We are doing great, just waiting for a table." Mark noticed Jake was holding a glass of beer, and probably not his first. He asked, "Are you old enough for that?"

Jake put a finger to his lips and said, "Shhh," looked towards the bar and said "They think I am." then winked. "Hey man, I was gonna tell ya to keep an eye on that little dog of yours. There's a pack of wolves around and they would eat your little doggie in one gulp. I seen them over by the boat launch."

"Thanks for the heads up but I haven't seen any wolves around yet," Mark said. "I thought I heard some coyotes but maybe it was wolves."

"I think they might have been in your yard, cause something was digging in that big snow pile I plowed up. I mean, something dug a big old hole, and I don't think it was your little dog."

Mark thought for a moment and asked, "Why would a pack of wolves dig in the snow pile?"

"I don't know, maybe I plowed some critter up in the pile and it died and the wolves dug it out? Hey, I gotta go, my girl looks a little pissed cause I'm not there talkin' to her, ya know?" Jake stuck his hand out to Mark and said, "Merry Christmas, shit, I mean Happy New Year to youse guys!" Jake walked away, stopping at a table to talk to some friends, ignoring the glaringly dirty look his date was giving him.

Sherry didn't like what she had heard. "Wolves? There is a pack of wild wolves in our yard? Why are they in our yard? What do they want, not my little princess. They aren't after my little princess are they? Can you shoot wolves?"

Mark finished the last of his beer and looked for the girl taking drink orders. He held up his empty glass and she waved acknowledgment of his order. "No, you can't shoot wolves, they are protected. The Department of Natural Resources is recommending a wolf season to thin them out up here but the tree huggers in Detroit voted it down. I think Jake is right, though, about them being in our yard. Something dug a hole in the front of Mt. Jacob. Maybe Jake did plow up a dead animal and the wolves got a whiff of it and dug it out."

"Well, what could it be?" Sherry asked.

"I don't know, a raccoon or maybe a skunk or something, but from the size of the hole it could have been a deer."

Sherry had a perplexed expression on her face, "Why would they want to dig it out?"

"To eat it," Mark answered. "The wolf pack probably dragged the body off into the woods and in a feeding frenzy, ripped the body apart carrying the parts throughout the woods. Anything not eaten by the wolves will be consumed by smaller animals and eventually insects until the rotten corpse is completely devoured, until nothing remains of the carcass."

Sherry said, "That's disgusting."

"No honey, that's nature's recycling program, nothing goes to waste, not even a dead rotten animal. But look at the bright side."

"What bright side?" Sherry asked.

Mark accepted his drink from the girl, ordered Sherry a refill and tipped the girl generously, wishing her a happy New Year then continued telling Sherry the upside of the wolves dragging away whatever they found in the snow pile. "When Mt. Jacob melts, I won't have to deal with the rotten, stinking carcass."

One man's pig is another man's wolf.

Thank you for reading.

Please review this book. Reviews help others find Absolutely Amazing eBooks and inspire us to keep providing these marvelous tales.

If you would like to be put on our email list to receive updates on new releases, contests, and promotions, please go to AbsolutelyAmazingEbooks.com and sign up.

Acknowledgments

Justin Maxwell is the name author Wayne Kadar uses when writing non-fiction. In this Justin Maxwell novel, the Wayne Kadar books published by Avery Color Studios; ***Rampage: Serial Killers, Great Lakes Serial Killers***, and ***Great Lakes Cold Case Files; Unsolved Murders of the Great Lakes Region*** are referenced. They are actual books and many of the murders in this novel are crimes taken from the Kadar books.

I want to thank Shirrel Rhoades, Chuck Newman and the rest of the staff at Absolutely Amazing eBooks for their continued support.

Since I was blessed (or cursed) with an overactive and unbridled imagination but developed little in the way of grammatical skills, I want to thank Karen Kadar, Sandi Skinner, Sue Scherman and Grant Kadar for bringing my writing into acceptable form.

And thanks to the Sunset Dock Crew, and all the people who have wandered in and out of my life for their inspiration and in some cases material to write about.

Meet the Author

Wayne "Skip" Kadar taught at the high school level for several years, then became a high school principal. After 16 years a principal Skip retired from education. In retirement he worked as a harbor master at a marina on the Great Lakes and researched and wrote eight historically factual books about the Great Lakes region; books about ships that now lie on the bottom of the freshwater seas. He also writes about notorious criminals from the region.

Mr. Kadar writes fictional pieces under the name Justin Maxwell so as not to muddy the waters for readers of his non-fiction Great Lakes regional books.

Now fully retired, Skip spends time with his wife, Karen, at the family cottage outside Manistique, in Michigan's beautiful Upper Peninsula, at their home in Harbor Beach, Michigan on Lake Huron and winters in the fabulous Florida Keys.

Other Justin Maxwell books
Available as ebooks or print

Tropical Dream – Nautical Nightmare

A group of friends decide to escape the cold Michigan winter for a weeks' vacation in a tropical climate and charter a boat for a warm weather cruise. They chose the Keys for a week of friendship and fun in the Florida sunshine. The three couples enjoy Mother Nature's best and one another's company until they cross paths with a couple of the sunshine state's more shady characters and their tropical dream turns into a nautical nightmare.

How the Mighty Have Fallen

When Jimmy and Emily hit rock bottom, losing everything, they took her uncle up on his offer of his 34-foot, 1963 Hatteras, Biscayne Beauty. It was a chance to start over. So off they sailed through the south end of Biscayne Bay to the Intercostal Waterway, ICW, which would lead them to their ultimate destination; Key West. Little did they know the danger that lay ahead, and the cache of diamonds that might very well be their ultimate undoing.

Life, Love and Sex of the Newly Single Adult

Due to divorce or death some of us find ourselves single and entering the dating world at a later stage of life. Follow Brian Demers on his journey as he learns how to deal with the life of the newly single adult. Brian vacations in Florida to escape the cold, snow and memories and to look for a life after Meredith. He meets old and new friends, some looking for companionship, and others who are trying to wring every drop of emotional, physical and sexual excitement out of life. He seeks the peace and tranquility of his Upper Michigan cottage to sort out his life and meets a crazy old coot called "Keeper", who is trying to restore an old lighthouse. Brian he gets involved with the project. Working on the lighthouse gives Brian's life purpose, it fuels his love for history, his love for woodworking, and before long it fuels his love for Keeper's daughter.

ABSOLUTELY AMA⚡ING eBOOKS

AbsolutelyAmazingEbooks.com
or AA-eBooks.com

www.ingramcontent.com/pod-product-compliance
Lightning Source LLC
Chambersburg PA
CBHW050356030726
47503CB00006B/1885